THE

GOOD

SHIP

First paperback edition by Stone Gateway Publishing April 2020

ISBN-13: 978-1-7340887-2-4

Printed in the United States of America

For my mother.

Thank you for showing me the incredible journey on every page.

"The ocean stirs the heart, inspires the imagination, and brings eternal joy to the soul."

~Robert Wyland~

CONTENTS

CONTENTS

THE

GOOD

SHIP

by

JEREMY M. WRIGHT

1

The Doorway to Eternity

The great scorching beast named July swallowed Annabelle Cross whole. It unhinged its jaws like a massive snake, slid its body in close for the strike, and finished its prey in a single gulp. In the belly of that monstrous beast, she was slowly, morbidly digested for all of eternity.

If I were to write a novel, it would begin like that. Those three sentences tell the entire story. The story of life on a boat. The story of life on the water. The story of life always reaching for a fleeting horizon.

The truth is that I've come to hate life on the ocean. I've never made a statement as honest as that. I loved it at first. When my father told me I would miss school to sail across the world, he was giving me exactly what I'd always dreamed. I was expecting to experience different cultures across each continent we briefly visited before moving on. A part of me also expected to see animals I've only known about from television or *National Geographic*. I suppose my expectations were much too high because the scenery never seems to change. It's always the same sky looming over the same water. It's desolate and certainly mind-numbingly boring.

I'm not saying that adventure was impossible to find in the middle of the Atlantic. It was a series of events beginning on a blistering July afternoon that gave me exactly what I'd searched for since we'd left port. The simple truth is what happened dramatically altered the way I view the world. Although I've traveled far in the last three years, probably more than any thirteen-year-old you might know, it's apparently a world I know absolutely nothing about.

Before our sailboat came in contact with the doorway of light, I thought that my dad and brother, Brad, and I have a pretty good handle on things coming our way. I guess we live by the adage of life handing you lemons, and you make lemonade and all that jazz. Now I realize how life has a funny way of delivering a swift kick to the brain when you're not even paying attention.

I'm usually focusing on a book, so what happens in front of the boat doesn't concern me. My thoughts are always a million miles away from my life on the water. After spending all this time traveling the seemingly same stretch of ocean, anyone would desire a mental break for a short while. However, today of all days, my attention is right where it should be.

The light was a hard thing to miss. It appeared from nowhere and hovered on the Atlantic's surface like some sort of beautiful doorway to Heaven. Tangled streams of multi-colored light moved across the opening in a strange, hypnotic dance that pulsed every few seconds like a heartbeat. Ribbons of light stretched toward us like eagerly reaching hands.

I shifted my focus from the light and watched my father as he battled for control of the boat. Beads of sweat trickled down his reddened face. He caught me watching him and shouted something. His voice drowned out by the light's whirring noise that sounded like helicopter blades chopping at the air.

It was either common sense or fear that made me stand from the bench, find balance, and carefully run toward the stern to my father's side.

"Why can't we turn away from it?" Brad asked.

"I've been fighting it. The sails are catching the wind just right, and I've been trying to steer around it, but nothing is working. Whatever this thing is, it seems to be pulling us in. You two hang onto something," my father said.

He continued to fight the ship's wheel, but his efforts couldn't match the hold the light has on us. When the bow hit the light, it released a shower of sparks and swirls of streaming light racing across the deck and wrapping around every surface of our boat.

A moment later, my father gave up the fight. He grabbed us and pressed us hard to the deck. His body protectively covered us from whatever might happen as the light surrounded the boat. My father's embrace was suffocating as I felt my ribs compress and the breath pushed from my lungs.

I was amazed that I didn't feel an electric shock as the light brushed my skin. Instead, I felt a tingle that seemed no more dangerous than the pleasant touch of the sun. Strangely, the sensation of the light was more calming than terrifying.

I opened my eyes and looked at the bow. I then looked at the stern and realized the web of light was now behind us. Our boat easily passed from one side to the other. Whatever strange phenomenon creating the storm of flickering lights appears completely harmless.

"That was unbelievable. I thought for sure the thing was going to electrocute us," my father said. He released us, and we all stood.

It was the moment when I noticed that our surroundings were different. A heavy gray fog stretched across the ocean. It wasn't only the fog that seemed to change our surroundings. Even the water we drifted was somehow different, blacker, and colder. I couldn't be sure. We watched the shifting fog with interest. Before the light appeared, we had smooth sailing as far as the eye could see. Now we were lucky enough to see fifty feet in any direction

"Where did this fog come from?" I asked.

"It wasn't there a minute ago," Brad said. He then quickly headed to the starboard side to vomit. He firmly held the railing and leaned dangerously over the side as he took care of business. Although Brad frequently suffers from motion sickness, I was sure that this time, it was the experience with the light which had rattled his nerves.

"What do you make of it, Dad?" I said in a nervous whisper.

"I'm not sure. I've never seen heavy fog roll in this fast. There must be a strong storm ahead of us. I want both of you to put on life jackets and stay close to me."

Although I'm a powerful swimmer, and I have no trouble keeping afloat beside the boat when Brad and I are allowed to go into the water, I did as he said. I know the power behind storms on the ocean. Storms out here can be an unforgiving force to battle.

I held out a life jacket for my father.

He waved his hand and said, "I won't need it, Annabelle. Have a seat right here."

"Take it, Dad. We're all going to wear one. What would happen to Brad and me if the boom knocks you on the head and you fall into the water and drown? What would we do?" I said sternly.

4

He smiled, took the life jacket, and said, "You sounded like your mother just now. You're right. I guess my stupid brain skipped a sensible gear."

"Sometimes it's the children who are smarter than the parents," Brad said, and then he slipped on a puddle and went down on his rear with a yelp.

"Well, that counts you out," I said after I finally quit laughing.

"Shut up, Annabelle!" he said while massaging his butt.

"Quiet, both of you," my father said while studying the fog.

"What is it? What do you see?" I asked. I curiously watched beside him.

"I'm not completely sure. I thought I saw something moving in the fog."

I wasn't thrilled to hear that. I may hate life on the water, but I greatly enjoy reading tales of the sea. Nothing gets my attention more than books filled with tragedy on the high seas. Now all of those fictional monsters were coming alive in my mind.

As we watched the shifting fog, a thunderous boom viciously rattled me down to my sneakers. There was an immediate flash of fire in the distance. A moment later, something with incredible velocity splashed into the water ten yards from the boat.

"What was that, Dad?" I said.

"It almost sounded like a—"

I thought my father was going to say: *cannon*, but his voice cut off because another explosion made the entire boat tremble. A second later, something collided with the bow of our boat. Whatever the object was, it made our ship deeply groan from the impact. The perfectly crafted wood gave little resistance to the hit.

The boat shifted hard, and Brad and I nearly toppled over the railing. We managed to grab each other and find balance before taking a swim.

"What's happening? What hit us?" Brad said as he released me. He moved to the center of the boat and took a firm hold on the mast.

"Are we sinking, Dad?" I asked.

I now had a terrible thought that the three of us would be floating in the middle of the ocean without a rescue ship in sight.

"Oh, my God. Another ship is attacking us," my father said. He quickly moved to the emergency kit hidden beneath the stern bench seat.

He removed the flare gun, inserted a silver cartridge, and then thrust his arm in the air and fired. A flaming ball cut through the fog and raced skyward. There was a small pop as the parachute was released. A shifting red glow fell across us as the light signaled to anyone nearby that we were here and in serious trouble.

"There are children on this boat! Hold your fire!" my father shouted as he waved his arms.

Then I saw it. We all saw it. Something massive slipped from the fog. It *was* another ship, but certainly not the type of ship I was used to seeing. I blinked a few times because I was sure the fog was playing tricks on my eyes.

As the ship moved closer, I realized that there was no trick about it. The ship was greenish colored and with tattered sails. Strangely enough, it resembled a pirate ship, as if it had slipped right out of the eighteenth century and into modern times.

I know, a pirate ship, it sounds ridiculous, but that's what I saw.

A roaring explosion followed another flash. This time the force of the blast knocked me off my feet, and I painfully slammed on my backside.

The port side was violently hit again, causing our boat to buck hard to the starboard side. Our boat then tilted as it took on water. We tried to hold onto something, but as the boat began rolling, we had no choice except to slip from the deck and into the cold Atlantic water.

My father continued to plead to the unseen men to hold their fire, even as water rushed into his mouth.

I swam toward Brad. His arms were flailing as he desperately searched for a hold of something. His brown eyes were wide as his focus switched from the sinking ship to my father and then to me. I got in close and managed to get a grip on his lifejacket.

"Stop thrashing and hold onto me," I told him.

Our boat continuing to roll as water completely flooded the ruptured hull. The mast, riggings, and sail crashed around us in a tangled mess. A dozen unsecured things flew at us. I never saw what it was, but something heavy catapulted from the deck like a hurled anvil and struck my forehead. The blow shot a roaring pain across my head, forced the light from my eyes, and pushed me into the grasping hands of unconsciousness.

2

Little Miss Lost

"Are you one of them? Are you one of the spies?" someone said.

A rush of saltwater ran in my mouth and up my nose. I pulled my head back from the sand and coughed wetly. I pushed myself onto my knees and carefully leaned back. I slowly ran my eyes up from the filthy feet to denim shorts and then to the torn and faded blue tee shirt. When my blurry eyes finally reached the face of that person, I saw a skinny boy staring down at me. He had medium-length dirty blonde hair, narrow green eyes, and deeply suntanned skin. He was studying me as if I were a strange sea creature that had washed onto shore.

I coughed again, wiped sandy, wet hair from my face, and tried to stand. My legs were wobbly, but they held me up. I looked at the boy for another long moment and then focused on the land behind him. I didn't see buildings of any kind or any other signs of civilization. There was a thick tree line running down the beach and nothing more.

"Are you?" he said impatiently.

"Huh?"

"Are you a spy? I'm usually pretty good about spotting them. Only I'm having a hard time figuring you out."

"A spy?" I said.

"Are you telling me that you don't know what a spy is?"

"My boat was attacked. It might have been a—"

His eyes brightened, and he said, "Were you on the boat that the Jade Army attacked? I knew someone would make it to shore! I just knew it!"

"—pirate ship," I finished.

I turned and studied the endless beach. "Have you seen my father and my little brother? They went into the water with me."

"No. You're the only one I've seen. Sorry, but the other two didn't make it to shore."

Tears spilled down my cheeks as I searched the crashing waves.

Instead of the filthy boy comforting me, he said, "Relax. You'll probably see them again."

"I don't understand. How can I see my family again if they're dead and lost at sea?" I said as I angrily wiped away the tears.

"Take it easy. Your father and brother aren't dead. They've become recruits for the Jade Army. I guess you're lucky, or maybe they didn't want you after all because you're a girl. No offense."

"You haven't made a bit of sense. Are you insane?" I said as I watched the boy's face for some confirmation to my question.

He held out his hand and said, "Let's start over. I'm Nathan. Everyone here calls me Nate for short."

"You said my father and brother are alive?"

"Shake my hand first, introduce yourself, and then we'll get to that."

I watched him closely for a moment before offering my hand. "I'm Annabelle Cross."

Nate smiled and said, "Nice to meet you, Annabelle. Like I said before, your family is alive. They're not in the best place to be right now, but alive. That's what you should be happy about."

"You better be right."

"I am. You'll see. I cross my heart on it. Come with me. I want you to meet everyone else. The others will be thrilled that another person has arrived. We haven't had a newcomer in years."

I popped the release on the life jacket, shrugged it off, and held it at my side as we walked up the beach to the tree line. I figured Nate's friends were somewhere in those dense woods.

"Who's the Jade Army? Are they pirates or something?"

Nate laughed, a soft chuckling followed by a sharp snort from his nose that made me smile.

"I never get tired of hearing that. Everyone who comes here says it the same way. Pirates. I suppose you could say they're pirates. All they care about is taking things that don't belong to them, and that includes people. Keeping us on this island is their job, and they're very good at it."

"How long have you been on this island?" I asked.

"I don't know. What year is it?"

"You don't know what year it is?"

"You'll see that time has little meaning in this place. Trying to stay alive is our first and most important goal," Nate said.

"It's July of 1965," I said.

He nodded. I saw a mild look of interest.

We stepped into the thick growth of the island's forest. As the trees and undergrowth closed around us, the sunlight faded to a dreary gloom. Despite the heat of the

10

day, I felt a chill come over me as we followed a narrow dirt path cut through the field of green. For some reason, I had a bizarre feeling someone or something was watching our movement through the forest.

Nate glanced over his shoulder and said, "Don't worry, it'll pass."

"What?"

As if he had read my mind, Nate said, "The eeriness of the forest. It's scary at first, but soon you'll figure out that some of the creatures out here are more concerned with protecting you instead of hurting you. If you talk about something, it might take your mind off of it until we get to camp."

I rattled my brain, looking for a question. I said, "Okay. Do you have any family members with you?"

"Only one brother. The Jade Army took my other family members."

"I guess it's pretty lucky that you have one brother with you. I wish my brother were here. Even though he's a major pain, I'd still like to have him here," I said.

"My brother, Max, is thirteen, a year younger than me. Unfortunately, he hasn't been himself in a long time. Max was in the forest collecting branches for firewood when he got bit by a black and blue."

"What in the world's that?" I said.

"Oh, a black and blue is a type of beetle. It's black, except for a pale blue mark on its back that kind of looks like a human skull. The beetle crawled out of one of the logs Max had collected, bit his hand, and gave him the seven-year flu. Stay clear of the beetles whenever possible. They won't bite unless they feel threatened," Nate said.

"Seven-year flu?" I said.

I've never heard of anyone having the flu for such a long time. For that matter, I've never heard of a black and blue beetle.

"Yeah, the gateway of light you went through brought you to a place stranger than from the one you came. There are a lot of weird things happening on this side of the gateway. Now that you've told me what month and year it is, I figure Max should be coming out of the illness anytime now. That's a good thing for everyone, especially him. We've all had to work in shifts to take care of him since the illness got so bad."

I thought about what Nate said. I had the flu two years ago. The sickness stuck with me for nearly a week. I remember how I felt like I was dying a slow and painful death. My head endlessly throbbed as if my brain were trying to escape through my ears. My nose hadn't stopped leaking. I coughed until my throat was raw and painful every time I swallowed. I also remember the full-body ache and cold shivers that never left until the fever finally broke. I couldn't even imagine experiencing something like that for seven years.

"Several of the other kids have suffered bites from a black and blue beetle, but their illness has long since passed. Max is the only one who's taken an illness this bad in a long time."

"I'm glad he's going to be all right soon. What's that?" I said.

The massive forest thinned as we moved into a partial clearing. What I saw was astounding.

Nate turned, smiled, and said, "Home."

3

All That's Left Behind

As it turned out, "*home*" was nothing short of a spectacular tribute to the human ability to construct a child's imagination. So it seemed to me anyhow.

My sight traveled slowly up the towering trees to houses high in the branches. Maybe not really houses, but more like small huts spotting the forest skyline. I counted at least sixteen, with two buildings to each tree. Wooden platforms circled each tree, and suspension bridges spanned the gaps between the trees. It was an impressive high-rise community. The scenery above was a mystical fortress that astounded me and brought on a series of exciting questions.

Someone built the huts using battered timber, cut to length and then secured by nails. The roofs were also constructed with wood and then coated with something that looked like tar to help seal out any rainfall. The boards and handrails of the bridges were bound together with nautical rope.

I stood at the base of one of the trees. My mouth hung open. My eyes were wide as I took in everything. I stood like that for several minutes before I suddenly realized that Nate and I weren't alone. I noticed dozens of eyes watching from the small windows of the huts.

My voice trembled a little as I whispered, "Who are they?"

"I suppose you could say they're your family now." Nate turned his sight to the huts above and yelled out, "It's all right. Her name is Annabelle Cross. She's just arrived. Her boat was the one we heard the Jade Army attack. They took her father and brother. She isn't a spy if you're worried. Come down and introduce yourselves."

A group of children began moving into view. Some of them were as young as five, and others as old as fifteen peered out the windows and doorways. Several children quickly stood from the cover of the bushes at the base of the trees. Some of the young boys held straight branches with one end sharpened to a point.

The children wore ratty clothing and their bodies covered with grime. It certainly looked as if they'd been here for a long time.

"Who built all this?" I asked.

"We did," Nate said. His face was beaming. He was certainly excited and proud to show every new arrival the town built high in the trees.

"Where did all these kids come from?"

Nate smiled. "Just like you, we all washed up onto the shore. The ocean spat us out."

"All of you live in the trees?"

"Mostly. It's much safer in the trees. You don't ever want to be on ground level when the sun goes down. That would be asking for trouble. We learned the rules of the island early on. You'll learn them fast, too."

"There are rules?" I said.

"Oh, yeah, but only if you want to survive."

"Survive?" I whispered. I wanted to survive, but I wasn't entirely sure why I should be protecting myself.

Nate turned his sight to the treetops and said, "Drop the stairs."

One of the boys pulled a knotted rope fastened to a handrail on one of the walkways. A long section of stairs slowly descended. On the opposite side of the tree, a large gray boulder tightly bound in rope steadily raced to the treetops.

Nate said, "I designed the pulley system that works as a counter-weight. The length of the descending stairs is a little heavier than the boulder. When the anchor rope is released, the stairs fall, and the boulder moves upward. Since the weight between the two is pretty close, it doesn't take much to pull the stairs up at night. You have to remember that the stairs always need to be up at night."

A cute, blonde girl that couldn't have been more than eight years old led a small group down the stairs to where we were standing. Her blue eyes carefully looked me over. Her attention fell on the bracelet I had made with my mom a few years ago. There were blue, pink, violet, and yellow strings woven together to create a spiraling effect.

"Pretty," she said in a sweet voice.

"Thank you."

"Can I have it?" she said.

I looked at my bracelet and frowned. "No, I'm sorry, this is one of the few things I have to help me remember my mother and how much I miss her. What's your name?"

"Melissa."

"I'll tell you what, when we get some time, and if I can find string we can use, I'll help you make one of your own. Does that sound okay?"

Her dirty face brightened. "I'd like that."

"I would, too," I said and brushed the hair from her forehead.

The children approached us, and one by one, introducing themselves. I was amazed that so many young people lived here without adult supervision. I was even more amazed to learn that many of them have been here for years. Somehow they found the determination to do whatever it takes to get by in this place. I was starting to understand what Nate meant by surviving.

"There are others besides us. Some of them work in the gardens, and others are somewhere else working on an important project. Let's head up the stairs, and I'll show you around," Nate said.

Before we began up the stairs, I noticed deep grooves scored on the trunks of the trees. It looked as if a massive animal had raked its claws against the trees, maybe attempting to climb up to the houses.

As we took the stairs to the lowest hut, I said, "What kind of important project are they working on?"

"I'll tell you about it later. Maybe tomorrow I'll even show you. I get excited every time someone new gets to see it." Nate waved his hand and said, "Never mind all that now. I didn't mean to build your curiosity. I want to start by showing you what we have here at base camp."

"This place is incredible. How long did it take to build everything?" I said.

"Years. I couldn't say how many. We've lost track of time so long ago that it doesn't have a purpose here. We work during the day and hide at night."

As we walked into the first hut, I looked at the few pieces of furniture. There was a constructed bed made from branches, and fastened between the supports was a thick fabric that I figured was a sail. There was a small table also made of branches and several flat planks. A small metal fire ring was below the window.

"Cozy," I said.

"We only worry about the bare necessities. In one of the buildings on the ground, we have a stockpile of clothing and other assorted things we share. Once a week, groups take dirty clothes to a freshwater stream and wash everything. We also use the stream for our drinking water, bathing area, and water for our crops. This island has everything we need to survive. Come on, let's head up to some of the other buildings," Nate said.

We went from one hut to another and one level after another. By the time we reached the last two huts, I had noticed how high in the trees we were. That was also the time when I saw how much the wind was rhythmically swaying the trees. I gripped the handrail and peered over the edge. We must have gone up five stories. The distance to the forest floor made me a little queasy. I stepped back on the narrow platform and pressed my back firmly to the tree. I closed my eyes and drew in a few long breaths.

I've always believed that redwoods were the tallest trees in the world, but these trees would tower over them.

"Please tell me that one of these upper buildings isn't where I'll be sleeping," I said and gave a nervous laugh.

"We'll probably construct a new building for you a little higher up," Nate said, as his eyes focused on somewhere far above.

I playfully slapped his shoulder when his serious look cracked, and he began laughing.

"You can stay anywhere there's room. We can even make you a temporary pad to sleep on the floor of my room, or I can take the floor, and you can have the bed. So you know, each group only stays topside for a week and then we switch job positions. We'll rotate in five

17

days. You'll be one of the recruits for our group. I think that should give you enough time to get to know the responsibilities we take care of on the island surface. Then we'll get to move to my favorite place of all," Nate said.

Island surface? I wondered. It seemed like an odd thing to say. Of course, so far today, I've traveled through a weird ring of light, and then our boat was blown from the water by a pirate ship. I doubted that anything else today would fall under the subject line of normal.

"Look at this," Nate said as we entered the final building.

The hut was crammed full of odds and ends. There was a small pile of worn-out electronics, a waist-high stack of battered clothing, a collection of weather-faded toys, and rickety shelves overloaded with tattered books.

I followed the narrow path. I studied the items with interest. I was amazed that the group kept some of the items even though there weren't use for them on the island. I searched through the torn clothing, most garments beyond holding a repair stitch. There were also piles of mostly broken electronics and toys.

The shelves held large amounts of novels and textbooks ranging from good condition to faded yellow and crinkled by water damage. I studied the titles on the spines. The authors spanned from Shakespeare to Jules Verne, as well as H.G. Wells and dozens of others. Of course, I've read most of the books. I've always loved spending my free time reading tales of adventure. Considering that I've spent years sailing across the world, I'd say that I've probably read twenty times more books than the average person my age.

I selected a thick book titled: *How They Were Built*. The cover showed an enormous ship battling a crashing wave. I flipped through the pages and saw brief images of different ships throughout the ages and each vessel's structural breakdown.

"I think every one of us has read that book at least twice. It's a favorite. You could say that it's required reading material. Now it's your turn to read the book. I'm going to give you a test at the end of the week."

I studied Nate and quickly realized he was teasing about the test. At least I thought he was teasing.

"What's with all this stuff? I understand why you're keeping the books, but everything else, like the electronics and other odds and ends, has no real purpose in this place. So why keep all these things when you could use this building as another sleeping area?" I said.

"Oh, that's where you're wrong. Everything here has a purpose. Every object has some sentimental value. These items remind us of who we were before we came here. You see this?" Nate retrieved a battered compass. I was pretty sure it had become so damaged that it no longer pointed true north. "This was mine. My father gave it to me a long time ago. He told me that if I ever got lost, this thing would help me find my way. Of course, in the old world, this might work, but not in this place. I don't think this compass has enough magic in it that would allow me to find my way back home. I think what's in your hands is far more magical in the ways of showing us the path back from which we all came."

Nate tapped the book in my hands. I looked again at the picture of a sailing ship fighting the raging sea. I didn't understand his point.

"You seriously want me to read this?" I said.

"Not only read it but study it. I want you to understand the structural layouts of the ships this book describes. I've just given you an important assignment. I'm serious when I say everyone has read that book several times."

I selected another book from the shelf and said, "All right, but when it gets boring, I'm going to read something else for a while. I promise I'll read this all the way through, even though it looks like a slow read."

Nate offered a warm smile and said, "Sure, I understand. I think after I show you something important tomorrow, you'll be more than excited to study that book. I'm not saying that I want you to memorize everything in there, but I want you to have an understanding of everything it takes to bring something from a page in a book and make it a reality."

"You lost me."

As Nate led me from the hut and back to the forest ground, he said, "Let's just say that there's something extra special I want to show you tomorrow."

"I hope it isn't another treetop that could make me lose balance and fall to my death," I said.

"No. We won't be going up. I'm taking you to a place that might fit somewhere in the pages of that fiction book you've got. We're going somewhere special. Trust me."

4

Tale of the Twin Sisters

After we finished dinner, which happened to be fish, I asked Nate to show me around a little more.

"There's a freshwater spring on top of the hill that makes a beautiful waterfall and collects in a small lake before it overflows and continues down into the ocean," Nate said.

"I'd like to see it."

A girl named Maggie followed us to the waterfall basin. She was ten years old, a cute blonde with eyes the color of the sea. She was chatty and full of energy.

"Could you tell me how my team is doing? The Red Sox, I mean. That's my favorite team of all," Maggie said.

"Oh, I'm sorry, I don't know. I haven't watched television or listened to a radio program for a long time. My dad used to be a baseball fan, but now he doesn't follow any sports since he changed jobs," I said.

"What does your dad do?" Nate said.

"Well, before my mom died, my dad was an attorney. When my mom got sick, my dad quit his job to take care of her. She passed away a little over three years ago. My dad got a new job sailing expensive boats from one country to another. Let's say that some rich guy in South Africa purchased a yacht built in the U.S.; well, the only way to get the boat there is by sailing it. I suppose someone has to do it. My dad's only one of a handful of people in the world that does that type of work."

"I think that's pretty neat. You must have seen every country there is," Maggie said.

"Well, not quite. We've only been doing it a few years. I've been to some interesting places so far, but I think this place has them all beat," I said.

"Oh, you haven't seen anything yet. You should wait for a few days. You'll see stuff that will blow your mind. Some of the things here would only be believable in tales of fiction," Nate said as we reached the crest of a hill.

"That's for sure," Maggie added.

As we broke from a mass of undergrowth, I saw, felt, and heard something spectacular. My mouth dropped as my eyes traveled up the cascading waterfall. An endless run of crystal clear water tumbled down the moss-covered rocks of the hill. There was a cool mist that crossed the small lake and gently sprayed us. I laughed with a strange sense of wonder.

"Come on!" Maggie called out. She kicked off her shoes, thundered down the shore, and collapsed into the water.

Nate offered a crooked grin and said, "I guess I should have told her there are piranhas in the water."

"Don't let him scare you, Annabelle. I've been in here hundreds of times!" Maggie called out while back paddling.

"You're mischievous," I said to Nate.

I quickly stepped up to him, grabbed his wrists, and spun him toward the water.

"Wait, my shoes," Nate called out. He tripped over his own feet and fell backward into the water.

I laughed as he floated on his backside, removed his sneakers, and tossed them at me. I dodged both projectiles.

I kicked off my shoes and sprinted into the pleasantly cool water. My legs lost speed when I was knee-deep, and I tumbled forward.

When I sprang up, gurgling a mouthful of water, Nate pounced and dunked my head down. When I came up again, Maggie had taken my side, and we were in full retaliation. Both of us attacked and sent him underwater.

Maggie and I laughed and declared victory.

"Can you tell me honestly if anything is swimming around us?" I said.

"Piranhas, I told you," Nate said.

"I wasn't talking to you," I said.

"I've been up here plenty of times. I've never seen anything in the water except the lights," Maggie said.

"Oh, no! Something has my leg. It's pulling me down!" Nate screamed as he thrashed around.

Maggie and I watched with amusement as Nate fought the invisible creature.

"Good. I hope it eats you whole," Maggie said.

"Still, we could at least try to save the helpless boy," I said and winked.

Maggie and I paddled toward Nate. He stopped flailing as we approached. We reached out and thrust his head beneath the surface again. Nate came up spluttering and splashed us.

After the war was over, we bobbed in the waves caused by the waterfall. I took a moment to enjoy the scenery.

"Is this the place where everyone comes to bathe?" I asked.

"No. There's a smaller basin down the hill we use," Nate said.

"So, you just come here to cool down and play?"

"Sometimes. But we also come here to dive for treasure," Maggie said.

"Yeah, right, treasure, I'm sure," I said.

"I'm serious. There's a ton of gold, rubies and diamonds and other things at the bottom," Maggie said with a convincing look.

"Oh, yeah? So how exactly did all that treasure get down there? Did it fall out of the sky?" I asked.

"No. This place is the secret lake of the Jade Army. When they attack ships and take the people, they also take any valuable possessions on the ships. They've been doing it for centuries," Nate claimed.

"Hiding valuables at the bottom of the lake sounds pretty stupid to me. So I guess that means you can't tell a truthful sentence," I said and then dunked Nate's head underwater again.

Nate didn't pop up right away. Instead, I had just enough time to catch a quick breath before something gripped my feet and pulled me underwater. I opened my eyes underwater and looked at Nate. He was pointing toward the foggy bottom of the lake. At first, I wasn't sure about what it was I was seeing. Something was faintly glowing in the murky darkness. I didn't think it was light reflecting off precious jewels or anything like that, but it was an incredible sight. I couldn't judge how far down the lake went, but I knew I could never reach it in a single breath.

I came up quickly as the glimmering lights below moved around. Whatever the thing is scared me a little.

"What the heck is that?" I shouted a little too loudly in Maggie's ear when I hit the surface.

"No one knows for sure what the lights are," Maggie said.

"Doesn't it scare you? Something is down there, and you're not worried that it might suddenly rise and grab you?" I asked.

Nate suddenly went under again. He briefly broke the surface, declared that something had a hold of him and that we should save him.

Maggie and I looked at each other and rolled our eyes. Boys could be so stupid sometimes. Instead of another attack, we swam back to shore and let the monster from the great depths have its afternoon snack.

Nate realized there wouldn't be a rescue after a minute, and he stopped his senseless splashing.

Maggie and I walked up the shore and began wringing out our shirts. We collected our shoes and waited for Nate to join us.

When Nate trudged up the bank, I said, "Really, what's that light down there?"

"It could be anything in a place like this," Maggie said while pulling on her shoes.

Nate said, "If you want to know, then I'll tell you about the old legends. There's someone on this island named Graur you'll eventually meet. Anyway, he once spoke of the legend of the twin sisters. It's a story passed down for generations. Centuries ago, there were twin sisters who were the rulers of this land. Their names were Lothlora and Simora. They weren't human but a creation that could take on any physical form they wished. As Graur explained, the sisters once ruled this majestic place far from the reaches of humankind. This place didn't use to be a bunch of islands but was once a large body of land filled with creatures like you've never imagined."

Nate led us down the path and back toward base camp.

"The twin sisters had entirely different views on how the land should be created and ruled. Lothlora felt that the lands didn't need to be controlled but watched over like silent guardians, only intervening when it was necessary. She suggested that the creatures of the lands understood basic survival. They needed to eat and breed to continue their existence. However, Simora felt that the lands needed constant order. She said that if all the creatures were able to do as they pleased, they would destroy one another. As you can tell, Simora didn't believe in the possibility of harmony."

"So, in your opinion, would you say Lothlora was a lazy ruler?" I asked.

"Not at all. I think Lothlora had the right idea. Simora wanted to prove to all the creatures of the land that she was in control," Nate said.

"Yeah, Simora had serious control issues," Maggie added.

"So, what happened then?" I said.

"Well, as you can imagine, the conflict between the sisters reached a maximum level. There was a great battle between them. Most of the things the sisters created are now gone. The power they used to build the lands had fractured. This division of power caused a huge earthquake that broke apart the land. That's why there are only a few islands left around here. The sea claimed everything else," Nate said.

I was impressed with his story so far. He certainly knew how to weave a tale together.

"So who won the battle?" I asked.

"Well, each sister shouldn't exist without the other, but when the battle finished, each of them still held a small amount of power. Simora fled to the woods. She built a dark nest and has been there since. Lothlora retreated to the depths of the lake we were just at. The glowing you saw is what remains of her."

"Nicely finished," I said. "I'm impressed that you added the mysterious light in the lake. That way, the story seems more solid, more believable."

Nate and Maggie curiously glanced at each other.

"I don't follow. What do you mean?" Nate asked.

"You put the story together pretty well. I probably would have thrown in a couple of different angles, but it was well done."

"No, Annabelle, it's all true," Maggie said. Her eyes were beaming at me, daring me to protest the facts of the story.

"Sure, I know. I believe the whole tale."

"Now you're the one being a liar," Nate said as he closely watched me.

"Okay, well, it might be a little out there. I mean, it's good, but a couple of god-like twin sisters who could take on any physical form, it's a little hard to believe," I said.

"It's all right. I know you've just joined us on our crazy little island. When the time comes, I'll willingly accept your apology," Nate said as we reached the edge of base camp.

"I have a feeling there won't be a need to apologize for anything. I think you'll feel the need to apologize to me for telling such a crooked story that isn't even in the least believable."

"I guess we'll just have to see," Nate said.

I asked Nate where the restroom area was. I tried to keep in mind that this wasn't a top-rated hotel on a majestic island suited for those sitting comfortably in the lap of luxury. The bathroom was a small shack with a deeply dug hole. I worked with what I had.

When I stepped from the bathroom, I spent a few minutes walking around and observing things. I had a hard time focusing on the wondrous things the children have constructed because my thoughts kept traveling back to my father and brother.

I reflected on the bizarre moments during the day. The thing made of light that ate our boat and the pirate ship completely flipped my world upside down like I never thought possible.

I was sure that things were only beginning to get strange.

I didn't think there was any possible way of preparing myself for tomorrow.

5

The Grouch Tree

The following morning Nate and I followed a carved path through the forest. I was curious about the destination Nate had in mind. I asked him before we fell asleep about what the children did during the day. I was quickly under the island's spell. There was no doubt that its mysterious and magical aura could capture someone's imagination seconds after stepping on the ever-expanding beach. However, I was sure that even I could quickly find myself dying of boredom. Each child I've met so far would need something to fix their attention before going stark-raving mad.

The island's mysteries, the exceptional children occupying the land, and the Jade Army's questionable motivation to guard the island's borders have dramatically increased by the hour. I desperately wanted answers that I felt I wasn't going to get.

"Hey, check that out," I said as I spotted a large tree to the left of the path. The trunk ran up as much as ten feet before the first row of branches started. Hanging in groups of threes from the upper limbs were round purple fruit of some sort, resembling baseball-sized plums.

"Hang on, Annabelle, you shouldn't step too close," Nate warned.

"They almost look like fruit. Have you ever had one?"

"Yeah, but only twice. When the fruit falls from the branches, you usually can't find them because the animals get to them first."

"Why don't we climb up and get them? The branches are only slightly out of reach. I could climb this small tree next to it and reach the lowest row of branches," I said.

"You're right, you could, but they don't like to be touched, especially by people."

I turned and watched him curiously. "Who doesn't like to be touched?"

He pointed. "The trees. Everything on this island we've given simple names, much like the black and blue beetle. We call everything as we see it and also by the way it acts. We call these grouch trees. They get highly agitated when something touches them or tries stealing the fruit."

I let out an amused laugh. I thought Nate was trying to make me believe that this island was capable of possibilities found nowhere else in the world.

"A grouch tree? Are you kidding me? So what exactly would the big, bad tree do to me if, let's say, I walk over and put my hand on it?"

"I wouldn't step too close. Trust me, Annabelle. Practically nothing on this island is what it seems to be. The fruit up there is probably the most delicious fruit you'd ever taste, but it certainly isn't worth your life."

My eyes traced up the tree to the fruit. The statement about being the most delicious fruit I'd ever have was mighty tempting. I walked to the trunk and playfully pressed my forefinger to the rough bark. I was daring Nate's strange fantasy to come to life.

I either felt something shift, or my imagination got the best of me. Through the nerve endings in my fingertip, I thought I felt a slight tremor. I pulled my finger away and studied the tree for a moment. After deciding it was my imagination and nothing more, I placed both hands on the trunk of the tree. I drew up a mental plan of how I would scale this behemoth to get to the fruit.

Not even my wild imagination could compete with what happened next. The ground beneath my feet came alive. A dozen small roots snaked from the earth, blindly searched the surrounding area, found my sneakered feet, and painfully curled around my ankles.

I felt deep panic grab me as I shouted, "Nate, Nate! Help me!"

The roots had a firm hold and began retracting into the dirt and pulling me along. I went off balance and fell on my rear. My left hand tried to find a hold of something as my right hand tried to unravel the tight grip the roots had on my legs.

Nate came down on his knees beside me. He removed his knife from the sheath and quickly severed the thin roots. Thicker roots exploded from the earth, but now their focus was on Nate. They attacked in large numbers as a dozen seized his arm containing the knife. In one fluid action, he tossed the knife to his free hand. With a single, powerful motion, he cut all the roots loose from his arm. Nate freed my legs with a few more swift strikes.

We began to retreat in a quick backpedal. The grouch tree made a groaning noise, and the entire thing trembled. It was as if the tree felt pain from the cut roots. Possibly it was a groan of anger at the two of us who had disturbed it for no particular reason.

The upper part of the tree bowed. I watched in disbelief as the upper branches bent toward us and harshly swept the forest floor. Small trees, bushes, Nate, and I collided with one large branch containing hundreds of smaller branches. We launched from the ground. Our feet and heads rapidly switched places while being flung a dozen yards away. We rolled in a heap along the dirt path and finally came to rest in the undergrowth.

I stayed still for a long minute. My left side flared with pain when I tried to catch my breath. I lifted my head and searched for possible damage. I didn't see any blood or arms or legs twisted at odd angles.

"I'm going to feel that in the morning," Nate said from somewhere in the mass of green.

I laughed a little, which was a mistake because the action caused my side to scream out.

"Lucky you. I'm already feeling it," I said.

Nate's head popped up. "Are you hurt?"

"I was just slapped by a tree. What do you think?"

He parted the thick growth and knelt beside me. He looked to the area I was holding. He pulled my hands away and then lifted my shirt high enough to study the lower part of my rib cage. He lightly probed each rib with his fingertips as if he were a skilled doctor trying to get an estimate of the injury.

"I don't believe anything broke. I'd call for a medic, but there's no telling how long it will take them to get here," he said and smiled.

"I'm glad you can have a sense of humor at a time like this," I said while holding back a giggle.

"You're for sure going to have one heck of a bruise."

"On the plus side, look at what I collected while doing three or more flips in the air," I said and pulled my left hand free from the tangle of weeds. I tightly gripped a cluster of purple fruit.

"I hope it was worth it," Nate said.

"I'll let you know after I take a bite."

"I also hope you're going to share."

I offered a sly smile and said, "Oh, I'm not so sure that I'm in such a charitable mood."

Nate held out his hands. I took them, and he carefully pulled me to my feet. The pain in my side wasn't nearly as bad as I thought it would be.

"Thank your lucky stars, because it isn't every day someone goes up against a giant grouch tree and walks away to talk about it. I'm surprised we weren't knocked right out of our socks and shoes," Nate said.

I wrapped my arm around his shoulders and used him as a crutch as we found our way back to the path.

"How can a tree move like that? Heck, it even knew our position. Do they have eyes and little brains to help them pinpoint the location of intruders?" I asked.

"I couldn't say for sure. I've never been that close before. Those roots certainly came to life as if the thing did have a brain. It knew what it was doing. It had some vague idea of what it would do with you once it had you wrapped up. I can't explain most of the bizarre things that I know about this island. There are strange days and even stranger nights. We only try to survive the best we can."

"Maybe the tree is like a Venus Fly Trap. You know, those carnivorous plants that snap shut when an insect crawls inside. Maybe those trees are meat eaters and quickly react when given the opportunity," I said.

"Maybe."

I twisted a fruit from the torn branch and handed it to Nate.

"Thanks," he said and quickly sank his teeth into it. Clear juice gushed from his lips. His eyes clamped shut. His expression lit up as the taste of the fruit awoken some emotional response that was nothing short of a delight.

I studied the fruit for a moment before I took a bite. Every taste bud came to life and danced. My entire body hummed with pleasure. My heart quickened, and my head got a little dizzy. Nate was right. It was one of the best things I've ever eaten. I thought just maybe the brutal slap from the grouch tree was worth it.

We traveled in silence as we ate. The quiet gave me time to reflect on the events I have so far experienced. The light, which had swallowed our boat, is some sort of doorway to a world unknown to the human race. It was at least unknown by those who have yet to travel the portal to this strange place.

Nate had told me that no one has ever been able to leave the island. If that were true, then why are there only children here?

"Do you think that perhaps the doorway of light could have different destinations?" I asked.

"So that we're on the same page, we call it a gateway, not a doorway. So you're wondering if it opens up somewhere other than offshore of this island?"

"Yeah. Do you think that maybe it swallows a ship and might very well spit it out somewhere random like other islands or even other worlds?"

Nate looked over his shoulder and smiled. "This place certainly has your imagination going. I've had many years to consider the purpose of the gateway. Everything I've guessed about it rounded me right back to where I was. We don't know anything about it, which's most likely the way it will always be. The only way I can view this island is by believing we're in some parallel universe. It's kind of like the world we left behind, mirrored in some ways and very different in other ways. I think that's the only way of accepting all of the strange things found on this island. I don't believe humans can understand something as fantastic as the gateway."

Nate was wise beyond his years. He has come to accept all things for what they are without questions or explanations. I have little doubt that he has seen things on this island that would boggle my mind. Something like that would make a young person grow up quickly. I thought that Nate had become an intelligent and remarkable young man.

After a challenging walk up the hillside, Nate and I broke through the foliage to a wide clearing. To the far south of that clearing was a stack of stones and a young girl with shoulder-length curly black hair. She was wearing a dirty and tattered yellow dress that had a long tear at the hem. Her feet were bare and looked toughened by the lack of footwear.

The girl casually watched us approach. She didn't smile, wave, or even speak as we crossed the grass-covered clearing.

I could hear the crash of the ocean waves nearby. I could even smell the salt-water in the air. I figured that just beyond the next cluster of trees would be the edge of the island and infinite blue expansion beyond that.

As we drew closer, I realized it wasn't a simple stack of stones but an entirely constructed circular well. Thick timbers were planted on opposite sides of the stones and then joined by a horizontal timber sitting on top. A sturdy rope ran up from the blackness through a pulley and then traveled twenty yards to a metal hand crank fixed to the closest tree.

I carefully peered into the still blackness and then studied Nate and the dark-haired girl.

"What's down there?" I asked.

Nate offered his winning smile. "I promised you something special. I always deliver."

"You expect me to go down there?" I said.

35

"Oh, yeah."

"You're late. You told me yesterday that you'd be here earlier," the girl said. Her voice was soft and stripped of emotion. She seemed bored.

"I know. We had a run-in with a grouch tree. Oh, sorry, Annabelle, this is Naomi. Naomi, this is Annabelle. The Jade Army attacked Annabelle's boat yesterday. I'm going to show her what we do here for entertainment."

"Great. Are you ready to go down?" Naomi said in an uninterested voice.

Naomi turned, followed the rope's length to the tree, and began rapidly cranking the metal wheel.

I wasn't sure of what to expect at the end of that rope. In this place, it could have been anything. What appeared out of that black void was what every person with logical sense would expect. It was a well-crafted water bucket.

"I'll go first and wait for you at the bottom. All you have to do is place your feet in the bucket and hold onto the rope. Naomi will do the rest. There's absolutely no reason to worry. It's completely safe," Nate said as he disappeared into the darkness.

6

The Secret of Darkness

"If you sit on the edge of the well and get your feet in the bucket, this whole experience will go a lot easier," Naomi said.

I needed my hands free for the journey down into the unknown blackness, so I offered the remaining fruit plucked from the grouch tree.

"Would you like to have this?"

The left side of Naomi's mouth curled into a slight smile. Other than that, her expression didn't change with the offer.

"Sure. That would be nice. You can leave it there on the edge of the well."

If she had only known what I went through to get the fruit, she might have been thankful.

Her hand was on the crank. With an amused look, she watched me comically manipulate the bucket with one outstretched foot, trying to hook the rope with my toes to bring it in closer.

After a few embarrassing moments, I finally managed to hook my shoe around the coarse rope. I pulled the bucket closer. I could have thought of a thousand different ways they might have set up this contraption so that it would have been easier for a person to avoid injury or death.

"Yeah, thanks. I got it now," I said with irritation.

My feet wedged in the wooden bucket. My hands took a death grip on the rope. For the life of me, I couldn't take my eyes from that black abyss and force myself from the safety of the solid ground. I couldn't stop the wheels of my mind whirling toward the possibilities of what lay hidden in that eerie blackness. What kinds of secrets were so great that they required a journey into a suffocating hole in the earth? The promise of something special was overpowering, but I still found myself resisting the urge to slide my rear from the wall and dangle above certain death.

"Annabelle?" Nate's echoing voice called from the darkness below.

"Tell me again that it's safe. Tell me again that it's worth it," I called into the well.

Nate laughed and said, "It's probably one of the safest things you'll do on this island. Trust me, Annabelle. Just let go."

I glanced at Naomi. Her face was a blank expression as if her thoughts were galaxies away. She was still poised in the same position while waiting for me to jump in feet first or turn yellow and retreat.

I trusted Nate, and suddenly I was swaying over the endless darkness. I heard the click-rattle of the crank as Naomi lowered me.

Unsettled nerves caused my body to tremble. The shaking caused the bucket to swing more than I felt comfortable. My backside bounced against the well's smooth surface, and then my nose ran across moss growing in the cracks. The bucket's bottom edge hooked the protruding stones several times, which caused the bucket to begin tipping. If I hadn't suddenly shifted my weight, which dislodged the hold on the wall, I believe the bucket would have upended and spilled me down the well.

"That's it, Annabelle. You're doing great!" Nate reassured.

I felt as if my journey had no end in sight. I glanced up and saw only a soft glow that was able to penetrate this deep. I also glanced down only to see the continuous and unwelcoming night.

"Please tell me that I'm nearly there," I prayed while pinching my eyes shut.

A voice answered after a long minute.

"Welcome, newcomer. We've been waiting for you."

When I opened my eyes, I realized that I must have been lowered right through the center of the planet and delivered right back to the open air. My eyes found the beautiful night sky. There was a vast black blanket, but spotted throughout the sea of darkness were sparkling, dancing stars. The bucket then thudded roughly onto a ledge of rocks.

I looked at the two boys standing there. One was Nate, and the other was a blonde boy holding a torch. He appeared a bit older than any of the other children I've met. The condition of his clothing matched everyone else's, which was ratty and nearly worn out.

I saw small fires burning brightly in the distance. As I turned around, I think I reached a full understanding of my current position. There was a rock wall running up to where the well's bottom hovered like a faint glowing halo. The space behind me opened dramatically into a massive cavern. I wasn't outside again. I was somewhere deep inside the island.

I stepped to the edge of the rock shelf and let my eyes take in everything. The area was as large as two football stadiums put together. The cavern ran nearly a hundred yards below our position, but the distance up was unknown to me. I suspected that it was most likely the distance I had traveled down the well, but for some reason, I had the feeling that there wasn't a ceiling in this spectacular place.

"My name's Malcolm," the blonde boy said and held out his hand.

"Annabelle Cross. Nice to meet you, Malcolm," I said. I shook his hand, but my eyes never left the view behind him.

"It's quite a sight, isn't it?" Nate said.

"Yeah. Where exactly are we, the center of the earth?" I asked.

"This is our sanctuary," Malcolm said.

"This is also the place where dreams come to life," Nate added.

"That doesn't explain much," I said.

Nate gently took my hand. It was a moment when I felt a spark of something extraordinary, something refreshing, and something unknown to me in my thirteen years of life.

I smiled shyly as our eyes met.

Malcolm rolled his eyes and said, "Oh, boy, I think we've got a love connection going on."

Nate, although younger and smaller, punched Malcolm in the bicep. Malcolm only laughed at the assault and threw his arm around Nate in a playful way.

"Relax, kiddo, I'm just messing around. Come on, let's show your girlfriend what we do down here at the center of the earth."

Malcolm took off down the rocky path to avoid another attack as Nate reached for him.

I could tell that Nate was embarrassed about the situation. I wanted to ease his discomfort as well as my own.

"I've never had a boyfriend before."

"Oh, don't you start, too."

I felt my face blush again. My eyes searched the area but kept returning to Nate.

"I'm serious. I don't think I'd mind that so much. My family hasn't settled in one place for long. I've forgotten what it feels like to have someone notice me. It's nice to speak to someone other than my father or Brad the Brat."

"Brad the Brat, huh?"

"Oh, you'd agree with that name if you only knew him. I know it's only been one day, but I do miss them a lot. I feel like a big piece of my life is missing."

"You'll see them again, I promise. When you see where we're going and the plan involved, you'll believe me."

"I believe you."

"Watch yourself. The path gets a little tricky farther down."

We cautiously maneuvered the twisting rock path worn down smooth from the constant friction of shoes and even bare feet walking this particular path for countless years.

I was watching my footing when Nate said, "Hold up a minute, Annabelle."

I stopped, turned to Nate, and said, "Yeah?"

"When you turn around again, I want you to look to the distance. More specifically, I want you to look between the fires out there on the cavern floor."

41

I did. What I saw out there made me draw in a sharp breath. Now I understood why all the secrecy. Nate's statement of a special promise couldn't have been more accurate. It was spectacular. What I saw was one of the most beautiful things my eyes have ever taken in. What I saw was hope breaking beyond the boundaries of limitations.

"What exactly is it?" I asked with astonishment.

"That's what happens when a dream comes to life," Nate said.

I remained careful as I followed the path in a sort of trance. The object in the distance captured my eyes. My heart began to gallop with anticipation at approaching the structure. I had to touch it to make sure it wasn't a fantasy at all but something of a reality.

When we finally reached the cavern floor, I approached the massive thing slowly. While my eyes made the long journey from bow to stern, I said in a dreamlike voice, "I'll ask you again. What is it?"

Nate offered a heartfelt laugh at my strange behavior.

"This is the Good Ship."

"The Good Ship," I repeated in a tone as if I were speaking in my sleep.

The ship floated on the rippling water, which filled a deep crevice on the cavern floor. Even with a dozen thick ropes securing the vessel to large boulders, the ship still gently rocked in the waves. Somehow they had figured out a way to flood this portion of the cavern to build the ship. I suppose the only confusing part was how they planned on setting the ship to sail when walls of rock surrounded it.

I slowly approached the dock. I walked the planks to a staircase running up like a fire escape on the side of a big city building. The stairs ran up more than three stories to the deck of the ship. To satisfy my mind and make the ship authentic, I placed my fingers on the hull and pulled my hand along the perfectly crafted wood.

I think Nate saw stars in my eyes because he said, "I take it from your expression that it was worth the trip down here?"

"Yeah, for sure. Who built this? Did you build it?"

"Yeah, well, myself and all the others. Everyone on the island has done their part in turning this ship from an idea on a piece of paper into an actual creation," Nate said.

"My God. How long have you been working on it?"

"Practically the entire time I've been here. It's been one long year after another. Your timing couldn't be better. After all these years, we're close to setting the ship to sail. In a little over a month, we're going to leave the island for good."

"That's good to know. I'm not usually known for good timing," I said.

I gripped the handrail of the staircase and began climbing. Nate followed close behind.

"It's huge. Why did you guys make it so monstrous?"

"This is our only chance to make a stand against the enemy."

"So, you made it strong enough to withstand an attack from the Jade Army?"

"Right."

"But they have powerful cannons. They blew my father's boat to pieces with ease. Well, my dad's boat wasn't anywhere near this big, but I think their guns could do major damage to even this thing," I said.

"We've made preparations for defense. You don't need to worry about that. We've had years to think up and invent all the necessary equipment we'll need to free ourselves from this place."

We stepped onto the deck, and immediately, my eyes took in the remarkable construction all the children have created. The view was a work of art, no, better than art because life imitates art or art imitates life or something like that. The point is, I felt at a loss for words. The ship was a fantastic creation not built by the hands of skilled craftsmen who worked a lifetime at the trade but by the desired hands of children.

"Where did you collect all this wood and the tools to build the ship?"

Nate fingered the fabric of a folded sail at the base of the mast.

"From the sea. We don't know how long the Jade Army has been blowing ships apart. Sunken ships fill the waters around us. The sea once took them, but we took them back. We collected nearly everything possible we could scavenge from those wrecked ships. Maybe soon I'll show you how we've collected all this material. It's quite an experience."

"Come on, show me around," I said and held out my hand for Nate to take it.

"I'd like nothing more."

Nate led me across the ship's deck, pointing out intricate parts combining into an enormous puzzle. He said a girl named Anica first conceived the idea for the ship. Anica was one of the first to wash onshore. Her boat had sustained severe damage during a storm before traveling through the gateway. She had been the only one to make it to the island.

I met several boys and girls on our tour around the ship. Each child seems to have a strong heart and an unbroken faith that the hard work they've been doing for countless years would break them free from the island.

The journey below deck was even more impressive. There were dozens of private rooms, a well-designed galley, and many bathrooms. There was also a common room that could comfortably hold a major league baseball team.

"Most of us now live on the ship or in the small camps around the cavern. Our fortress topside was our first effort at survival. We built those treehouses as a way of besting the numerous threats we faced every day. There are no enemies down here. Nothing in this place will harm you," Nate said.

"Then why do some of you still live up top?"

"As you can see, this place is a barren wasteland. Nothing grows here. There's very little here we can use to help continue our existence. We rotate groups each week. The ones who are up there now tend to the gardens and collect firewood that we also use down here. They also go into the sea to rummage the sunken ships, as well as monitor the beaches."

"That's a lot of responsibly."

"Yeah, it is. I do enjoy my time topside. I love to feel the sun on my face, but down here is where I truly belong. I've put so much blood, sweat, and tears into making the ship what it is. I suppose we all have. I think each of us feels a certain connection with the ship. It's part of who we are and how we've grown during our time on the island."

Nate led me back to the deck. When we walked to the stern, I saw an attractive girl with straight black hair and an olive complexion. I thought she was maybe a few years older than me. She was facing us, waiting for us to approach. She offered a warm smile as my eyes met hers.

She held out her hand, and I shook it. It was a simple, civilized habit from the old world.

"Annabelle, I'd like you to meet Anica. She was the first one stranded on the island. She's also the strongest, smartest, and most mentally collected person on this island," Nate said.

"Nice to meet you, Anica," I said.

"I hate it when you introduce me like that, Nate. How hard is it to say, 'Annabelle, this is Anica'? You make me sound like some divine presence. I'm just a girl with a few good ideas. Got it?" she said and then poked Nate in the ribs.

I laughed at her attempt to embarrass Nate.

"I'm just trying to boost your self-esteem because someone mentioned you didn't get enough beauty sleep."

Even though Anica is slightly smaller than Nate, she could hold her own. She playfully charged, gripping Nate's forearms while entangling his legs, and they crashed on the ship's deck, laughing.

After a brief moment of wrestling, Anica was sitting on Nate's stomach, her hands pinning his arms to the deck.

"Uncle?" Anica asked.

"I let you win."

"Uncle?"

"All right, uncle. I give, I give."

"Good, because it's time for lunch," she said.

"I still have a lot of questions," I said when the laughter died away.

"Fire away," Anica said as she stood and helped Nate to his feet.

"Well, first of all, what exactly do you eat down here?"

46

7

One Millioŋ aŋd Oŋe Questioŋs

Sometimes you ask questions to which you don't want the answers. Whether or not I wanted the answer this time, I got it anyway. Lunch, as it turned out, was an odd assortment of sea creatures. Some I've seen before. Some I've eaten before. Some were strange sizes and shapes that made me cautious about the flavor. Some had the appearance that promised excruciating pain to my inner workings if I dared a taste. Since the children have survived for so long on the things offered to me, I trust they knew the safe to eat creatures from the harmful ones.

Nate was watching me with an amused grin. I knew he could detect the uncertainty in my decision of what to try first.

"You might like to know that fifteen children have died trying different foods to find out which ones are poisonous and which ones are safe. We've figured that these are okay for most of us, that's unless you're allergic. The only way to know for sure is to try it and see which ones make you deathly ill," Nate said. The grin never left his face.

I pulled my hand away from something resembling a crab, but it had two more sets of legs and a few more eyes than the ones I've seen.

"I'm not hungry after all," I said.

"Come on, Annabelle, I'm just kidding. No one has died eating any of the food here. You need to loosen up a little."

"Are you trying to get yourself in trouble again?" I said playfully.

We gathered food on our plates and headed to the main deck. Nate said he always ate on the deck when he was in the cavern. We found a seat on one of the folded sails and quietly ate our meal. I enjoyed everything I had chosen from the small buffet. Nate instructed me on how to crack open the shells to get to the meat inside. He showed me which parts were the good stuff to eat and avoiding the guts since my stomach wouldn't agree with the offer.

When I had my fill, I placed my plate to the side and stood. I walked to the stern and studied the three cannons. These weren't constructed of iron like traditional cannons but had once been thick tree trunks. They were about six feet long and nearly two feet in diameter. Four steel bands wrapped around each cannon for added strength. The kids had somehow managed to bore a six-inch wide hole down the center. I was sure that somewhere around here were cannonballs to fit perfectly. The children of the island never cease to amaze me.

"Tell me about this place," I said.

"Sure. What do you want to know?"

"Everything. Okay, for starters, what makes the cavern ceiling sparkle like that? When we first came down here, I was sure we were outside again, only it was suddenly night, and the stars were out."

"Um, they're a type of crystal. They're all over the place. The crystals reflect the fires from the different camps around the cavern, which makes it appear as if

48

they're twinkling stars," Nate said. He licked his fingers clean and stared up at the fantastic natural creation of the cavern.

"Okay, my next question might seem dumb to you, but remember that I just got here, and I haven't the slightest clue on how things work around here or the plans behind them. What method do you guys have planned to get this ship out of here and into the open water?"

Nate slapped his forehead and said, "Oh, man, I knew we forgot something! It was so stupid to overlook that!"

"Knock it off, wiseguy. I can very well see the ocean can get in here. So that means we're a short distance from open water. So how on earth do we move something this gigantic through the cavern wall and sail for freedom?"

Nate smiled at his silly behavior. He pointed to the cavern wall that was only fifty yards from the bow, made his hands into fists, and then quickly spread his fingers as his hands moved apart.

"I'm no good at charades. Do you think you can tell me in English?"

Nate shifted his gaze over the railing and to a boy who was probably a little younger than me. The boy was sitting on a boulder at the port side, a lunch plate in his hands. His bare feet moved back and forth in the gently rippling water.

"That's Cody. He's the kid with the plan that will set the Good Ship free from this cavern."

"Okay, I'm interested. Keep talking. How has a young boy like that created a plan that will move this massive ship out of here?" I asked.

"Well, you see, Cody's our explosives expert. That entire wall is loaded with enough charges to bring it crashing down and allowing us to set sail. Of course, that isn't everything there is to our escape, but that's how the wall will come down."

I pointed to the boy. "That kid's an explosives expert?"

"Well, he hasn't blown up himself or anyone else. So, he's the elected expert," Nate said.

"Crazy," I said with astonishment.

"We've been blasting away at that wall nearly as long as we've been building the ship. The cavern floor beneath the ship had naturally eroded long before we came here. The area is a great deal lower than the rest of the cavern. It was Cody's idea to start using explosives to allow the sea to fill in the void below us so that we could build a ship in a makeshift port. Enough time and blasting finally brought the sea in, allowing us to start building the ship. Cody's idea has two strong points behind it. First, it offers shelter from weather conditions so we can work on the ship anytime. Second, and most importantly, the cavern allows us to keep the ship a secret from the Jade Army. If we had a dock somewhere on the beach, they would easily blow the ship from the water at first sight."

"The element of surprise. I like that. It sounds like Cody's pretty smart."

"He's one of many. We all have our specialty. After all the blasting, we've determined that the wall is now only a few feet thick. If we blasted anymore, the whole thing would probably come crumbling down before we're ready to go, and our secret would be exposed."

"So, there's going to be one last explosion when everything is complete, and then every child on the island will finally be free?"

"That's what it comes down to," Nate said.

"I believe a group of children who built something impossible to sail past the Jade Army with little or no confrontation and race for our home will be a day to remember," I said.

"Don't forget about the precise timing needed to sail into the gateway and teleport ourselves back to our world. That's a big issue for us. You see, the gateway moves like it's on a time clock. There's nothing random about its destinations. It appears and disappears with set intervals and locations. We've spent years documenting the locations of the gateway and its distance from the island. We know the exact day we have to blow the wall down and set sail to reach it before it vanishes again."

I turned my sight to Cody. He had finished his lunch and was now walking along a worn path beside the ship's dock. He seemed bored, even unchallenged at this moment. He appeared like a boy waiting for something big to happen.

"What are the odds that this plan will go smoothly?" I asked.

"There's nothing smooth about it. It's a complicated dish to swallow. Kind of like those sea urchins you ate if you had left the spines on. It's certainly a triumph or bust situation that no one here can calculate the results. All we can do is make our move when the time is right and hope for the best," Nate said in a tone of confidence but tinted with doubt.

"So, how can I contribute to making this plan successful?" I said.

"First, we need to discover your special skill, and then we put you to work."

"Sounds fair. If I have a special skill anyhow."

"You do. We only need to coax it out of you," Nate said.

"Tell me about the Jade Army. Who are they? What makes them do the things they do? What's their purpose of blowing ships from the water and kidnapping crewmembers from those ships? What do they gain by keeping us here on the island?"

"The girl with one million questions," Nate said as he offered his now-famous smirk.

"One million and one," I corrected.

"I'll give you all those answers. Well, to the best of my knowledge. Right now, I want to take you around the cavern to the camps. I want you to meet everyone. We certainly don't want anyone thinking you're a spy and torture you for answers you don't have. Besides, we've got to kill a little time because I want to show you something topside that you can only see at dusk. It's quite a sight to take in. Then we'll talk about the Jade Army and the purpose behind their madness."

8

The Irrelevance of Time

I must have met nearly thirty boys and girls as Nate and I explored the cavern. We stopped at each camp, and he introduced me. I liked each child I met. I did think it was odd that everyone seemed so nice. I didn't detect a hint of deviousness from a single person.

I remember the days when I attended school. Each year my classroom was filled with kids. Out of those students, there would have been several kids I wasn't friends with at all. There would have also been several kids I downright couldn't stand.

I realize at this point that I didn't have any negative feelings toward a single person I've met here. Strange, I know.

I took a long glance back to the Good Ship as Nate and I reached the peak of our climb. I admired every piece of the well-crafted ship. I also greatly admired that it stood for freedom and pride.

"Okay, just like before," Nate said as he helped me into the bucket.

"Maybe my special skill could be building an escalator so that we can do away with the rope and bucket contraption," I said.

"A what?"

"Escalator."

He shook his head, apparently not getting the joke.

"See you in a few minutes," Nate said. He gave the rope a tug, which told Naomi I was ready to go.

I went from the gloom of the cavern to the warm embrace of sunlight. I noticed the sun was making a steady race for the horizon. I didn't realize how long we had been down there. I figured sunset was maybe an hour away.

When Nate reached the surface, he nodded thanks to Naomi and said, "We're the only two coming up. You better head back to camp for the night."

"Sure. Are you coming?" Naomi asked.

"In a little while. I want to show Annabelle something," Nate said as he grabbed my hand and then led me toward the sea cliffs.

"You better not take too long. It'll be dark before you know it. By the way, thanks for the fruit, Annabelle," she called after us.

I smiled and waved to her.

We followed a path through the trees. I could tell this trail was rarely traveled because the plant life had nearly reclaimed the thin snake-like trail.

"This is always the best part of the day to watch the ocean," Nate said.

We came out of the trees and to the cliff's steep edge at the southern end of the island. Below us were the pounding waves against jagged rocks. It made me a little dizzy from staring straight down while watching the constant motion. Nate told me to sit near the edge, be quiet, keep my eyes and ears open, and enjoy the wonderful gift of nature.

I didn't want to ruin the moment or bring out Nate's irritability by my constant jabbering about nothing in particular. After a half-hour of silence crept by, I began to understand why Nate had brought me here. I started to feel a steady peacefulness come over me as I watched the breathtaking view accompanied by a swelling and rhythmic crash of the waves below.

"Can you see it now?" Nate asked. His eyes hadn't left the blanket of blue.

"See what?"

Nate pointed to a specific section of the ocean. At first, I couldn't figure out where he was trying to direct my attention. After a few minutes of studying the area, I saw the fantastic sight Nate had hinted at earlier.

What stretched out before us was a long, winding field of green among the vast blue. As the sun reached the western horizon, the darkening water's green glow became more pronounced.

"Oh, Nate, it's wonderful! I've heard of this before, but I've never actually seen it. That's incredible!"

"What you see is a massive trail of bioluminescent plankton. There's an undercurrent running from miles out. You can see how it twists toward the southern part of the island and then out to sea again. It's the same path that saved my life so many years ago."

"So, your ship went down at night, and the bioluminescence showed you a path to the island?" I asked.

Instead of answering my question, Nate asked a question of his own.

"What's an escalator? You said earlier that you might be able to build one."

I narrowed my eyes, waiting for him to crack a smile. Nate stared at me, waiting for an answer.

"I was making a joke. It's mechanical moving stairs that take you up or down. They aren't very common, but most people at least know about them. How is it possible that you don't know that?" I asked.

Nate was idly staring at his hands in his lap. His eyes seemed sad for some reason. He appeared like a boy burdened with more worries than a kid his age should.

"Annabelle, I was born in March of 1898. Back in our world on the other side of the gateway, I should be sixty-seven years old now. I've been a fourteen-year-old for a long time. For whatever reason, time is irrelevant here. Every kid you've met on this island, even the younger ones, were born years before you."

"How's that possible?" I asked with disbelief.

Nate shrugged. "It's one of the mysteries of the island. This place isn't bound by rules that you've come to expect in the other world. This place has strange, illogical methods of life we don't understand at all."

I looked away from Nate and to the green glow of the plankton. What Nate revealed was a hard kick to the part of the brain where logic resides. I usually would have rejected this conversation on the basis that Nate must have fallen when I wasn't looking and received a hard knock on the head. However, the tone of his voice and the earnest look on his face confirmed he spoke only the truth. I wasn't enjoying this conversation, so I felt the need to change topics until I had more time to sort out this information.

"How many people from your ship went in the water?" I asked.

"I don't know for sure, a few dozen. The ocean waves overtook some people. Some people might have even gone down with the ship. The Jade Army also took their share. I never knew what happened to my parents. I'd rather like to believe that they died when the ship went down, instead of believing the Jade Army took them into their collective clan of hatred."

"I'm sorry to hear that's something never answered for you," I said.

Nate gently took my hand and said, "You know exactly how I feel. Your dad and little brother are now lost, taken, or otherwise. Somehow I have a feeling that we'll be reunited with our families. It's just something I feel deep in my bones. I can't explain it any better than that."

"You don't have to," I said.

After a pause, Nate continued.

"Then there were only four of us floating in the ocean darkness. Luckily, we each managed to get a lifejacket when the ship was going down. We thought for sure either sharks or the ocean depths would eventually take us. After an hour in the water, the ocean around us began to light up in a brilliant green glow. This glow showed us a path to an island we didn't even know was there. We spent one exhausting hour after another swimming. We didn't know it was an island. We just knew it was land of some sort, and we were thanking God for it."

I watched Nate closely. I could see sincerity and goodness in his heart. As it turned out, his heart suffered the same aches as mine. In a sort of strange way, I felt like our loss connected us.

Nate's hand still held my own. His pale green eyes found mine. There was something there I've never felt before. Whatever it was, it made me nervous and exhilarated at the same time.

Nate moved closer to me, and I met him the rest of the way. My heart began a frantic gallop as our lips gently pressed together. It was a moment eagerly seizing us.

Nate's left hand caressed my cheek and then slid into my hair.

I couldn't say if it were the combination of the beautiful scene before us and sharing stories or if it was just something meant to be. Whatever the reason behind it, I had no complaints.

"That was nice," I said when we parted.

Truthfully, I felt a little embarrassed. Nate probably would have seen my face turn a deep shade of red if the sunlight hadn't been so faded. It was my first kiss, and I suspected it was probably on the extreme side of amateurish.

"I agree. I wasn't expecting it, but I'm glad it happened," Nate said.

After a moment of uneasy silence, I decided to break the tension by throwing in a wisecrack.

"Ugh, gross! I just realized that I kissed a really old guy!"

Nate started laughing. He stood and pulled me to my feet.

"It's getting dark. We need to get going. It'll take us twenty minutes to find our way back to camp. That should give us enough time before the forest is completely dark. Whatever you do, Annabelle, don't ever get caught in the open in the dark. It's a beautiful and even magical island, but it also holds sinister creatures that have no problem tearing a young girl like you to pieces," Nate warned.

"Just like a typical boy, spoil an uplifting mood with gruesome words of wisdom."

Nate laughed again and then led me down the curving forest path.

9

The Moving Night

"We've got to hurry. We spent too much time at the cliffs. Now the sun is quickly falling," Nate said.

We left the ocean view, the well acting as a doorway to the Good Ship, and the other children behind. We found the path cutting through the undergrowth and were making a hasty rush to safety. I followed close behind Nate's lead.

I briefly thought of the claw marks I had seen on the tree trunks yesterday. I planned to ask Nate about them, but I became caught up with everything going on, so I had forgotten.

"You never told me what exactly made those claw marks on the trees at camp."

"Something I pray you never need to face."

"Come on, tell me. I should be ready for whatever this island throws at me," I said.

"There are scavengers on the island. We don't know if they're part of the Jade Army or if they're simply on their own, looking to survive by all means necessary."

"So, there are children on this island who aren't members of your group?" I asked.

"No, not human at all. It's like black shadows with teeth and claws. Thankfully, I've never seen one up close.

Anyone close enough to get a good look at them has been taken and has never returned. We've been cautious over the years to stay clear of the forest grounds when night falls. No one has been taken in over a year, but it doesn't stop the hunters from trying to climb the trees to get at us. We'll be safe as long as there's still daylight. I've never seen them out during the daytime. Maybe the sunlight hurts or scares them. I don't know for sure, but they run wild during the night."

I stumbled over a fallen branch in the path and crashed into Nate's backside. He managed to keep himself upright and quickly seized my midsection to save me from a painful fall.

"Sorry. Thanks."

"Careful, we don't have time to nurse injuries," Nate said as he picked up the pace again.

"What do you call them? You guys seem to name everything here. You've got black and blue beetles, grouch trees, and the Good Ship. What simple name are these scavengers called?"

"Well, Anica calls them *a noite em movimento*, which means 'the moving night' in Portuguese. The rest of us call them the hunters."

"Where do they take the children they've managed to capture?"

"We don't know for sure. It's the common belief the hunters eat the children. Maybe death is better than anything else they might offer. I try not to think too much about what happens to those taken."

A few golden rays of the sun still broke the forest covering, but the darkness was beginning to loom with a stronger purpose of leaving us stranded in harm's way. I couldn't remember how long our journey to the well had taken earlier, but I suspected we were still quite a distance from camp.

Nate suddenly stopped and studied the area to our left.

"What's wrong?" I asked in a whisper.

"Shh. I thought I heard something."

"You better be messing around. If you're trying to give me a scare for the fun of it, then I've got some serious words for you."

Then I heard movement in the direction we were staring.

Nate removed the knife from its sheath and said, "Run as fast as you can, Annabelle. I'll be right behind you. Go, go!"

I did. I felt my legs scissor beneath me faster than they have ever traveled. I chanced a glance back and saw that Nate wasn't following like he had promised but had instead left the path and stepped into the thickness of the forest. His sight focused on the point where the movement had occurred. Nate readied his knife for a possible attack from the unknown creature.

"Come on, Nate!"

"Keep going. The path will lead you to camp. I'll be there in a moment."

I did as he instructed. I quickly concluded that Nate was a person who has grown to be a courageous young man needing to prove his nobility, or he was a typical stupid boy who let his curiosity get the better of him. In either case, I knew his extended entrapment on this island made him far more intelligent and cunning beyond his teenage years. There was still enough daylight to keep him safe from the grip of the hunters. I was sure that he would be racing behind my lead after only a moment of investigation.

When I chanced another look back, I realized that I was completely alone. The shadows reached long fingers across the forest grounds. The daylight that was here only a minute ago had given way to the unstoppable night.

I halted on the path and called out, "Nate?"

The only response I received was a rustle of leaves to my left. I turned and watched the area for movement. My heart was hammering so hard I could feel it in the hollows of my ears. Something was slowly walking through the sea of green and shadows. I could see the forest growth part as something passed below the surface.

I began to run again. That was until something large sprang from the covering and darted into my path. My safety was now in serious jeopardy as the path was blocked by something resembling a large coyote or wolf with eyes glowing like green fires. It didn't attack but calmly walked the trail toward me.

"Well, well, what have we here? Something delicious, I think."

It had taken a confusing moment to realize that the raspy, nearly demonic voice had come from the creature in front of me.

"Excuse me? Are you speaking to me?" I asked in a trembling voice.

"Well, a simpleton is what we have, I suppose. Who else would I be speaking to?" the thing said.

As the creature approached, my feet became tangled, and I went down onto my rear. For the life of me, I couldn't find the strength to stand up. The act would have been pointless anyhow. Whatever this thing is, it was fast and would take me down after only a few strides. I could only watch in disbelief as this wolf-like thing stepped dangerously close and spoke to me a language I clearly understood.

"What do you want?"

"Want? Oh, sure, I can understand your confusion, little one. The night is nearly upon us, and I've worked myself into a fierce hunger. There isn't much meat on those bones of yours, but I suppose you'll have to do until something bigger comes along."

It moved close enough that I could smell its breath. White fangs on its upper and lower jaws extended well beyond the reach of all its other teeth. I could see something resembling a small horn jutting from the skin of its muzzle behind the black curve of its nose. Its ears were large and cupped, most likely to catch even the slightest noise. It was a perfect predator of the night.

Its pinkish tongue slid across all those teeth with relish. It was an action telling me that it would be feasting on my insides any moment.

As the beast took another step, Nate suddenly broke from the casting night with his knife in his right hand and a thick branch in the other. The creature's head snapped toward the movement as Nate brought the branch down with surprisingly gentle force. The branch rapped smartly on the top of the creature's head. It released a high-pitched whine and cowered instead of launching a defensive attack.

"That's enough, Graur. Can't you see she's scared stiff?" Nate said.

"I'm sorry, Nathan. I was only having a little fun with my new friend. You know very well I meant no harm," the creature said, appearing to be somewhat shamed as its green eyes drew to the ground.

"I know, but you're having fun at someone else's expense. Annabelle doesn't know you or what you might be capable of doing. I was telling her about the hunters when you showed up," Nate said as he helped me to my feet.

I stepped behind Nate and out of reach from the creature that now seems as docile as a rabbit.

"My greatest apologies, young lady. Sometimes the animal instincts find the surface in all of us. I hope you didn't hurt yourself when you fell."

"Uh, no problem. No, I'm fine, just a little confused," I said as I brushed the dirt from my shorts.

"Okay, Annabelle, as you've just discovered, there are even talking animals on our crazy little island. I should have told you before, but I wasn't sure how much strangeness you could deal with today after our tangle with the grouch tree. Sorry," Nate said.

The creature bowed its head and said, "I'm pleased to meet you. My name is Graur. I'm a friend to all of the children here."

"Yeah, he might have seemed like a ferocious lion at first, but I assure you that he has the heart and temper of a pussycat. Graur's the one who told us the story of the twin sisters I shared with you at the lake yesterday," Nate said.

Graur's large ears suddenly pricked up, and his head lifted as he studied something behind us, something hiding in the curtain of shadows.

"Speaking of the hunters, young master, I believe both of you should make haste to your home. I don't think we're alone anymore," Graur said.

We both turned. The distant sounds of something drawing closer to our position got both of us ready for a fast race to camp.

"I wish you well, my friends," Graur said. His powerful body parted from our side, and with one swift leap, he disappeared as quickly as he had arrived.

The final touch of the sun faded from this part of the world and left us in utter darkness. As the forest seemed to close in, I felt a surge of an overwhelming panic build. I couldn't see the path in front of us any longer, so I relied on Nate's mental compass to guide us to a protective shelter.

As we saw the glow of fires in the trees, Nate began to yell.

"Hey, lower the stairs! Lower the stairs!"

I saw a dozen faces appear in the windows of the huts.

"Please, lower the stairs!" I called out.

I could hear protests among the group of children.

"No, Ella, the hunters will follow them up the stairs and tear us to pieces!"

"I said to lower the stairs. Do it," another girl's voice responded.

As Nate and I raced to the base of a tree, I thankfully heard ropes creaking as the counterweight raised and the stairs lowered.

"Go, go," Nate said as he urged me faster up the long flight of steps.

"Now! Raise the steps!" someone called out before we even reached the top.

The counterweight and the stairs began reversing positions.

Something unseen, something with impressive strength, launched itself into the air and managed an iron grip on the ascending staircase. Under the extra weight, the stairs were falling again. Something ravenous wanted up here. Whatever these things were, they now had the opportunity to sink their teeth into the children who have avoided them for so long. In the moment of terror, I felt a brief sadness that Nate and I were the cause of this entire ordeal. We were the reason that innocent children were going to die.

When we reached the top platform, I almost walked directly into a burning torch. No, that wasn't right. I realized it wasn't a torch at all. I instinctively pulled back from the flames. What I saw at that moment was Ella positioned in one of the windows. In her hands was a drawn bow, and loaded in that bow was a brightly flaming arrow. She released the burning arrow into the night. As the arrow cut through the darkness, it made a soft thud as it found a target at the bottom of the stairs. The flames grew as it ignited whatever monster was down there.

The stairs quickly began to rise again as the creature released its hold. I could hear the whimper of pain as the arrow had parted flesh, and now the flames burned. I saw below a strange dance of fire as the creature ran and rolled, desperately trying to extinguish the flames. That's all I could see, the fire and nothing more.

A moment later, the panicked rolling of the creature stamped out the fire. In the rage of the moment, the creatures below began attacking the base of the trees. I heard the rake of claws on the bark and the deep-throated growl of animals working into a fury. By the sound alone, it appeared as if the entire forest floor was alive with creatures. I could hear movement all around. The base of each tree with huts high on the branches was under attack by the creatures. There must have been dozens of them.

Nate and I moved into his hut and sat on the edge of his cot. A fire burned in a small metal ring at the opposite end of the room. Neither of us said anything. We stared into those dancing blades of orange and yellow and waited for everything to pass.

The clan of children in the trees kept quiet as we all patiently waited for the terror to end.

After nearly an hour, the forest night grew silent.

"I think the hunters have finally gone. They know they can't get up here. They've tried countless times. I think they were mad about not getting a hold of us when they had the chance," Nate whispered.

Ella stepped into our hut, followed by several other children.

"You better mark this day, Nate, because this is the only time I'm going to save your life. If it hadn't been for the others agreeing to drop the stairs, you and your new friend would be dinner for the hunters right now. They could have gotten up here, and everyone would have died," Ella said sharply.

Nate only nodded and lowered his head.

"It was my fault. I urged Nate to show me the way the ocean illuminates at dusk. If you want to be mad, then be mad at me," I said as I stood and approached Ella. It was a lie. I thought it was easier for the group to be angry with me instead of Nate.

Truthfully, I was shocked that someone Nate has known for years would so easily give him up to the hunters' horrifying hunger.

"Has the island completely stripped your humanity?" I said to Ella with sudden anger.

"This island has taught me to survive, girl. If the hunters had taken both of you, it certainly would have been a tragedy. You should always keep in mind that two lives aren't worth the dozens you see here. You better figure out all the rules quickly if you want to be one of the survivors when the time comes to leave this place."

Without another word, Ella turned and left the hut. The other children gave us disappointing glances as they followed Ella's lead.

When we were alone, Nate said, "She's right. I was stupid. I almost got the entire camp ripped apart by the hunters."

"It was both of our faults, but you can see that everything turned out all right. No one was hurt."

"Yeah, this time. All it takes is one bad choice that gets someone killed."

"We've learned a hard lesson today. We won't make the same mistake again," I said.

I was trying to offer Nate a way of accepting our major blunder this evening. I could see the ordeal was tearing him up inside.

It seems as if I'm having one heck of a time trying to fit in. Of course, that goes without saying wherever in the world I am, or even apparently whatever dimension I'm in.

10

Mischief Happens

As time went by, the children forgave my ignorant actions that nearly got the entire camp torn apart by the hunters. It had taken several days, but by the end of the third day, I was pretty sure I had befriended most of the children at base camp. Even Ella seemed to simmer down from the other night, and she finally began speaking to me.

I exchanged life stories with all of the children who spent time with me. I was fascinated by everything here. I was especially interested in the incredible tales of survival under the extreme determination the Jade Army showed at capturing them.

What I found the most interesting was the point in history at which each person vanished. At first, I found it difficult to believe Nate's story he shared at the cliffs as we watched the fantastic twilight view. Honestly, I didn't believe him at first but acted as if I did. I couldn't hurt his feelings if he were completely looney, and no one had yet to share this information with me. He wasn't crazy after all because I believe he told me the simple truth. Okay, *simple* is purely a loose term here. The truth was totally complicated and downright confusing.

I have trouble accepting how people could be on this island for decades, and no one has aged past childhood.

I have a hard time accepting Nate's basic explanation that time is irrelevant here. It wasn't an explanation at all, but more like a simple observation. It was apparent that no one grew older, but I wanted to know why. That's something about my character I've never been able to take lightly. When something found my interest, I wanted to know everything about it. I needed to understand how and why certain things worked here. So far, no one has given me a more clarifying answer. It isn't like this island comes with an instruction manual.

During the day, a group of us worked in the crop fields. I was immediately impressed with the layout and hard work tending to the crops. For a large group of children, they managed to grow the necessary crops for survival. Most of the children were city kids on the other side of the gateway who knew little about farm work.

The fields consisted of corn, beans, potatoes, tomatoes, and watermelon. These were the fields I've so far seen. Nate told me there are several more crop fields south of base camp. The fields weren't gigantic like the nearly endless acres of crop fields I've seen in the States, simply because the island has few flat open areas.

Although the children figured out how to have year-round fruits and vegetables, meat is no longer a food source on the island. Because of the creatures' unique abilities, the children decided there would be no senseless slaughter of any animals. So any creatures used for food would always come from the ocean.

Nate and I loaded a couple of baskets with some goods that should last a few days. When we figured we had collected enough, we turned toward base camp, and I stumbled over my own feet. I went down right on top of the wicker basket.

"Oh, jeez, are you all right, Annabelle?" Nate said as he helped me up.

I had a difficult time balancing myself. I looked at my feet. Somebody deliberately tied my shoelaces together.

"You're rotten, Nate. That practical joke could have hurt me. I hope you're happy that I squashed some of the vegetables I collected," I sourly said as I crouched and began working the knots free.

Nate started laughing a moment after he saw the triple knots worked into my laces. Listening to him laugh at me like that made me want to throw a few tomatoes his way.

"That's real gentleman-like," I said.

He held up his hands in surrender and said, "I'm sorry for laughing. It wasn't me who tied your shoes together. Honest. The same thing happens to everyone here once in a while. As we're all working, we tend to forget to watch our feet and the stuff we bring along with us. Around here, it's best to keep all your things strapped to you and to check your feet every time you're ready to move."

"What on earth are you talking about?" I asked as I finished properly tying my laces.

"You've had *mischief* at your feet. That's who did it."

"Who did it?" I asked irritably.

"Mischief, that's what we call them because they're a constant nuisance. Sometimes the mischief is amusing when those little guys do something especially clever," Nate said.

"I'm still not getting it."

"Well, they're small, probably only about the size of my thumb. The mischief looks like fairies that you might find in children's books. They have wings just as fairies do, but they can't fly around. Most of them are too fat and

71

can't get very far off the ground. Don't let that fool you because they're incredibly hard to catch. I don't believe they have much to keep themselves busy, so I think their main entertainment source is irritating us in the worst possible way. For the most part, they're harmless."

We gathered the spilled vegetables and started down the cornrow. Something in my peripheral vision flashed along the ground in the next row. Whatever it was, it was racing ahead of us. I saw one of the cornstalks move as the small body shimmied up it.

When we reached that point, I said, "Hold on, my shoe came untied again."

It was a simple but effective diversion. As I knelt, my eyes searched the cornrows. I quickly reached between the corn leaves and snatched the tiny creature. Because it was so small, it almost worked free from my grip, but I held on to the wiggling thing.

"Wow! I've never seen anyone reach right out and grab one like that," Nate said.

We studied the creature called a mischief. Strangely enough, as Nate had claimed, the little guy did look like a fairy. He was an angry, spitting ball of fury but a fairy all the same. He was chattering unintelligible words at us. It probably would have sounded the same if I had lightly clicked my tongue at him.

After a moment, he quit his struggling and eyed me with a look of innocence. He looked cute with his big brown eyes and locks of curly blonde hair. He was wearing brown pants and a shirt most likely made from human clothing. He also wore a hat made from a green leaf that was neatly folded and almost looked like one of the paper boats my brother used to build.

"I'm not going to hurt you, I promise. We only want to know why you little guys do the things you do to us?" I asked the mischief.

He began barking at me in a language I couldn't understand. He was waving his free arms around and pointing at the both of us. I thought maybe I offended him by calling him *little*. From what I could figure out by his barking and clicking, I thought he was trying to tell us that we were intruding on their property. Of course, I was only guessing. He could have been telling me the sky was falling, and I should take cover.

"Well, whatever the problem is between us, I'm sure we can reach some understanding. We never meant to take over any land that may have been yours. We're sorry, and we hope you can forgive anything we might have done to your people," I said.

Although I knew *people* certainly wasn't the right word for them. I couldn't think of another substitute without offending him more. For a moment, I couldn't be sure if he understood a thing I was trying to get across. Then he offered a crooked grin and gently patted my hand. His nearly transparent wings twitched a few times. He then sank his needle-like teeth into the pad of my thumb.

"Ouch!" I cried out and opened my hand.

The mischief dropped to the ground and took off like a lightning bolt. All we could see was a thing no bigger than a mouse scurrying across the cornrows. A devilish laugh was all that remained of the creature.

"Yep, mischief is probably the best name for those guys. I hope they don't carry rabies or any other kind of disease," I said as I inspected the small bite mark. There were a few tiny dots of blood, but nothing severe.

"No, you'll be fine. I probably should have warned you that mischief tends to bite."

"Yeah, a warning would have been nice. On the upside of things, I think I made myself a new friend," I said.

"I certainly saw a friendship connection there," Nate said sarcastically.

We returned to base camp and handed over our collection of food to Rose. She immediately began preparing for dinner.

Nate and I parted a short while later. He told me he would join up with a couple of his friends on the beach and do childish boy things. I told him that I'd hang out here and do silly girl things.

I found Melissa a few minutes later. She was the adorable little girl who I met when I first came to the treehouses. I remember how she loved the string bracelet I had made with my mother. I'd told her I could help her create one as soon as possible. Now I had some time to spare.

We went up to the hut that was the highest in the trees. It's the place that made me nauseous when Nate first brought me here. It's the hut where all the children stored special items from a life beyond the gateway. Melissa and I spent a while pulling free loose strings from some of the battered clothing. I didn't think anyone would miss them.

We sat in the hut she shared with two other girls. It was nice how just the two of us could get away for a while, make colorful bracelets, and talk.

I told her about briefly catching a mischief. I laughed when she said that I should have squashed the little bugger. She told me about all the trouble they've caused everyone over the years.

"How long have you been here?" I asked.

She shrugged as she focused on correctly looping the strings of the bracelet.

"What year is it?"

"It's 1965," I told her.

She did calculations in her mind and said, "Well, I came here in 1942. So it means that I've been here twenty-three years."

It wasn't easy to understand exactly how someone who was born well before me could now be younger than me. This little girl has been eight years old for twenty-three years. On the other side of the gateway, she'd be all grown up, thirty-one years of age, working a dream career, and most likely married with children.

"Are you looking forward to going home?" I asked.

She smiled nervously and said, "This is the only home I know right now. I'm excited and scared at the same time. I sometimes wonder when we go through the gateway if we might return to the time each of us originally came. I wonder if we'll remember anything we've done here. I hope to remember everyone, the island, and all of the things I've done. To forget any of it would completely suck," she said.

Melissa was a smart girl with many questions.

"I suppose when we all return through the gateway, we're going to get answers, but they may not be the answers we necessarily want," I said.

"I finished!" She triumphantly held out the perfectly crafted bracelet for me to inspect.

"Nicely done. I bet everyone will be jealous that you can make these, and no one else can."

"I'll teach them if they'd like to know," she said.

I smiled. Melissa is such a cute kid. It was at this moment when I thought of what she had said about returning through the gateway. Would all of the people suddenly be transported back to the time from which they left? Was something like that even possible? Of course, everyone vanished while on the water. Does it mean one hundred people traveling back through are pulled from the Good Ship and dropped into waters from the time in which they came? It was a possibility that terrified me.

When my father, brother, and I came through, we were still on our boat on this side. However, there was only one ship that was going to journey back through. There was going to be one ship and dozens of different locations and points in history that the gateway would supposedly propel us. Of course, everything was speculation at this point. No one knew the real purpose behind the creation of the gateway. I thought what I said a moment ago was going to be pretty accurate. I didn't believe any of us were going to like the answers we got.

A short while later, someone called out dinner was ready. Children came in from all around. I found that I was enjoying seafood more and more. I selected half a dozen shrimp, a fish I couldn't name, a slice of watermelon, and an ear of sweet corn.

"Tomorrow, I want to take you somewhere pretty cool. I think you'll enjoy it," Nate said around a mouthful of crab.

"Pretty cool? You know, for a kid gone from the real world for such a long time, you're still up to date with the lingo," I said.

Part of me was a little scared, and the other part exhilarated with Nate's mysterious destination in mind.

"Don't tell me that you have another ship being built in a secret cavern somewhere else on the island?" I said.

"No, we don't have a fleet we're building around the island. We only have one ship. I want to show you where we get most of the materials to build all of the things we do. It's extraordinary," he said, offering a sly, crooked grin.

"Extraordinary? Now I'm expecting to be highly impressed when you pull out a word like that," I said.

11

Into the Blue

The following morning I opened my eyes to find someone hovering over me. I quickly blinked a few times to clear my eyes and tried to focus on the face. At first, the boy seemed somewhat familiar, but I wasn't sure if I had met him before.

"You're right, Nate, she is cute," the boy said.

"It would be nice if you could avoid embarrassing me, Max," Nate said.

I sat up from my bedding on the floor. My mind began working in the early morning hours. Now I recognized the boy. I had seen him several times, either sleeping or stumbling around camp. The boy was Nate's younger brother Max. He was the kid bitten by a black and blue beetle and infected with the seven-year flu. Max looked altogether like a different person. He was now bright-eyed and freshly bathed.

I smiled at him and said, "Nate said that I was cute?"

"I won't comment further on that. I can tell by Nate's blazing red face and the steam coming from his ears that the pot is ready to boil over. It's a look like that telling me that his threshold of patience is near collapse," Max said.

"Don't worry about him. I'll tie him up if he gets too worked over. It's nice to finally meet you now that you're not in such a terrible state," I said.

"I remember that you're Annabelle. I remember many things during the last seven years, but I can hardly remember some things at all. I have to tell you that having the seven-year flu was kind of like I was aware only half of the time," Max said as he shook my hand.

"Well, I'm glad you're all right now. You look a million times better. I can't imagine what it was like to live with the flu for seven years."

"Pray that you never will. Anyway, I feel great. I'm starving. I'm going to get out of here, get something to eat, and a little exercise. It was nice to meet you, Annabelle. I'll see you two later," he said as he left the hut.

"Bye," I called after him.

"A couple of the kids woke me last night. They told me his fever was breaking. I can't believe he finally came out of it," Nate said.

"That's a great thing," I said.

"Are you prepared to start the day's activities?" Nate said while offering a smile that told me something wicked was in store for the morning.

A short while later, Nate and I stood on the beach. Water ran up the shore, curled around our ankles, and then retreated. I was staring into that hypnotizing stretch of blue. There was something about the ocean that I both loved and hated. The ocean is a mysterious thing in which I could never have the mental capacity to figure out. The ocean has its deep secrets, and it won't give them up to the likes of us. Count on it.

"Are you ready?"

"Ready as I'll ever be," I said.

"Help me get the boat in the water, and we'll paddle out to the area I have in mind."

We slid the small craft into the rolling tide. We struggled for several minutes as we fought the breaking waves but finally managed to get the boat on calmer waters. As we paddled toward the area Nate wanted to scavenge, I suddenly had an unsettling feeling that something watched us. I rotated my sight across the surface of the water. I had an overwhelming fear that the Jade Army ship would appear out of nowhere and fire its cannons against our small boat.

"Please tell me again that this is safe. Tell me that the Jade Army isn't going to show up and ruin my day in the worst possible way. Tell me that I'm not going diving for things we don't need. Will I run out of oxygen and drowned?"

"You know, you've got to be the most nervous person I've ever met. Does your mind automatically draw up the worst-case scenario during every situation you're in or what?" Nate asked as he glanced at me over his shoulder.

"I only think that this dinky boat is a death trap. That rig I'm going to be breathing through looks like a third-grade science project. Don't start acting like you weren't scared the first time you did this. I know better than that."

"Okay, okay, you're right. I was maybe a little nervous the first time I did this. I'll help ease your mind and tell you that it's perfectly safe. When you're below the surface, you'll be amazed at the sights down there. It's like another world."

I looked over the edge of the small boat. The water was a sparkling clear blue. I could easily see the bottom of the ocean, which was at least twenty feet now and increasing as we headed farther out. I thought about all of the sunken ships down there. This place is where groups came to dive and reclaim what the ocean had once taken. The material collected from here is how the Good Ship was born. Plank after plank was long ago removed from these waters, transported down the well, and put to use. It was once a necessary expedition into potentially dangerous waters.

"Okay, here's the deal, this isn't like your ordinary diving rig. This hose you use when you need a breath. Put the end of the hose in the water. I'll show you what I mean."

I took the end of the long rubber hose and placed it in the water.

Nate said, "Now, when I start pumping, these billows will draw in air, and when I press them down, air will transport through the hose to you. Watch this."

Nate used his feet and began pumping two things in the boat that looked like accordions. I had to smile at the action because it looked as if he were peddling a bicycle that was going nowhere. The air did just as he claimed. I saw a stream of bubbles coming from the end of the hose.

"That's pretty neat," I said.

"Yeah, I wish I could say it was my invention, but it wasn't. Before we had this contraption, we had conditioned our lungs to hold our breath for nearly four minutes. We'd take a deep breath, dive, and work at a site for only a minute before being forced to surface. As you can imagine, trying to salvage wreckage took a long time that way. Of course, back then, we could only work in shallow waters. Now that we have this, we can stay down there a great deal longer and go deeper. Put on the belt attached to the hose. It keeps the hose close at hand. You don't keep the hose in your mouth because you'll blow up like a pufferfish. I usually swim with the hose in one hand. Hold your breath and take air from the hose when needed. I'll constantly pump the billows until you come back up," Nate said.

"What are we scavenging for today?" I asked as I fastened on the belt.

"We're not looking for anything in particular today. We have most of the supplies we need. We've already cleaned out the ship below us. I just wanted to bring you out here and show you exactly how we've been able to recover all the stuff from the sunken ships. If you happen to spot anything you like, feel free to grab it and bring it to the surface. Put these on and then put these in your ears," Nate said, as he handed me a pair of blue snorkeling goggles that looked well used and two small pieces of rubber.

At first, I didn't understand the purpose of the rubber pieces. I then realized Nate wanted me to use them to safeguard my eardrums from the pressure of the deep.

I put the goggles on, adjusted the strap, and worked the rubber plugs into my ears. I slipped from the boat and into the pleasantly warm water.

"By the way, if you happen to see any sharks, punch them on the nose when they get too close. That usually startles them away. Have fun," Nate said in a joking tone. At least I hoped it was a joking tone.

"Great. When that doesn't work out, I'm going to poke you in the eye with my stump," I said and then splashed him.

I took a deep breath and sunk below the surface before Nate countered with another wisecrack. The air bubbles immediately began rushing from the end of the hose. I was a little worried about how well this breathing method was going to work. I decided to give it a try before I swam too deep. I released my breath and drew in fresh air from the hose. It was a little weird at first, but the system worked pretty well.

I rotated my body and began kicking toward the ship below. Nate was right about this being an entirely different world. Don't get me wrong, I've seen some incredible things beneath the surface of the ocean, but I never had the chance to explore the wreckage of a ship graveyard. Even from this distance, the sight below was an incredible thing to take in. The boat directly beneath me looked as if it went down only a few years ago. The ship was still in the beginning stages of being devoured by the ocean.

I could see several more sunken ships not too far away that appeared decades old. The metal parts now remained savagely rusted, as the salty ocean water has eaten away at the ships for years. The pieces of wooden decking left behind were covered entirely in coral and seaweed.

After a minute of swimming downward, I reached the ship that had already given up its treasures to the island's children. I studied the remains of the wreckage. I spotted a gaping hole near the bow and swam toward it. Several of the hull planks were torn or blown away. I swam through the opening and made sure the air hose didn't hang up.

As I carefully made my way into the ship, I noticed a distant glowing spot from another ruptured hole in the side. I released my breath and received another from the hose. I watched with interest at this hovering bright dot in the distant waters. It swirled through the water like it was doing a strange dance. I didn't have a clue what the thing was, but I was certainly curious.

The ship itself was impressive, but the children had reclaimed everything necessary long ago. Now the boat was only a rotting structure of metal and wood.

The glowing dot was quickly joined by two, three, and then as many as ten more spinning yellow friends. They seemed to team up and then did a mesmerizing display of seemingly choreographed moves.

I backtracked my passage through the ship as I followed the trailing airline to the place I had entered. I carefully gathered the slack of the airline in my arms. I stood on the broken ship and watched those lights dance.

I've never seen sea creatures like these before. These fantastic creatures are probably only found on this side of the gateway. For whatever reason, this place contains creations found nowhere else. Because of that truth, this place is so fascinating to me. I'm one of the few people who get to witness the existence of creatures only considered something of a fable in my world.

Something large moved in the distance to my right. I quickly turned my sight, only to catch a glimpse of a long, pale orange beast swimming close. It had been heading toward me, but when I turned, it shifted direction with an agility I've never seen before. It was there one second and gone the next.

I rotated to view the water around me. I could see the glowing dots but no other movement. Suddenly I felt a little dread creep into me. The situation reminded me of a poorly filmed scary movie.

My imagination was building the fear inside. I took another breath from the hose and swam for the surface. As I ascended, I fully expected a tentacle from below to curl around my leg and pull me into the deepest reaches of the ocean.

I broke the surface, and with Nate's help, I flopped into the small boat.

After a minute, I finally adjusted my breathing from a panicked state to a comfortable rhythm.

"I saw some weird things down there," I said.

"Yep, I would guess so. You probably saw only a small fraction of what these waters contain. There are some things out here that your mind would have a hard time believing," Nate said as he reached down and twirled his fingers in the water.

"I saw these yellow lights. It was like they were dancing with each other."

Nate smiled. "No, they weren't dancing. They were feeding on the plankton. Now that I think about it, I guess it does look like they're dancing."

"I also saw something else. I only saw it for a brief second, but it was huge. It was moving toward me until I turned to look at it, and then it swam away. It scared me half to death. I thought it was going to grab me."

"Huge? Would you say that it was the size, shape, and color of something resembling a giant squid?"

"Yes. Exactly," I said excitedly. "You've seen it before?"

"Then I'd say you're lucky. Anyone who has ever seen that beast before died terribly."

I stared at Nate for a long moment. Then something clicked in my mind. I punched him in the shoulder.

"If that were true, then how would anyone living know about it if everyone who saw it died?"

A smile cracked, and Nate rocked back with laughter.

"I almost had you on that one! I suppose you're finally catching on that I'm full of wild, good humor."

"You're full of something all right, but it isn't good humor. That thing seriously scared me," I said sourly.

85

"Relax. All of us have been in these waters countless times. We've all been down to the shipwrecks. There isn't anything swimming in these waters that have ever hurt any of us. Those things that look like giant squids, I don't think humans are on their menu."

"That's good news because the thing was certainly big enough to crush this little boat and snack on us if it wanted to," I said.

"Have you had enough of an adventure for today? Are you ready to head back to shore?"

Even though I believe Nate's statement about no person ever being harmed by the creatures in these waters, I still felt vulnerable in this tiny boat.

"Yeah, I'm ready to head back. Thanks for bringing me out here. It was certainly an experience I won't ever forget."

Nate offered a gentle smile. "I know, Annabelle. I've been on this island for many years. I've had so many experiences that I'm sure I'll never forget. I think that if we're able to return through the gateway, I hope the memories stay with us. There's so much about this place that I'd never want to lose."

Although I've only been on this somewhat magical island for just under a week, the memories I've collected so far are now priceless to me.

12

Lessons to Learn

The week finally came when our group switched places with the group working on the Good Ship. There was no denying it, but being below in the cavern quickly became one of my favorite places on the island.

It may seem strange to some that a dark, musty cavern with only sources of light by campfires, torches, and candles would be such a wonderful place to be. For some reason, this is the place in which ninety percent of the children preferred to stay. There's something majestic and inspiring about it. It's a place where hope thrives the most.

I patiently waited for days to get back here. Don't get me wrong, I love learning and experiencing all there is about tending to the crops and scavenging ship wreckage, but this is the place always on my mind. I eagerly waited for the moment when I'd be lowered into the well again. I desperately wanted to be shown exactly how the children created the ship. Now I have an entire week to learn everything I could before rotating to the surface again.

"Okay, one of my million questions is about what you use as explosives. Does there happen to be a sunken warship off the coast once filled with barrels of black powder you were able to get to shore?" I asked as we came down the slope leading from the bottom of the well.

"Not at all. It isn't black powder. The explosives have grown right here on the island. Follow me. I'll show you."

We approached the rock wall separating the Good Ship from open water. Nate opened a large wooden box, pulled out a four-inch-long black stick, and handed it to me.

"Wow, thanks, I didn't get you anything," I said sarcastically.

He took my elbow and led me to the nearest campfire, where several kids worked beside the fire. Kyle was gently carving on a board with a small hand tool while Lizzy braided string together to make a rope.

"Could I get both of you to move aside for a moment?" Nate asked.

They saw the stick I held and hurried away from the area as if I had the plague.

Nate watched me and said, "Go ahead and toss it in."

I started to walk closer to the fire, but Nate grabbed my shirt and held me back.

"I think this is as close as you want to go. It actually might be a little too close."

We backed up another dozen feet. Nate gave me the okay nod, and I launched the stick at the fire. It flipped through the air, landed dead center, and lay there.

"That's quite the magic stick you gave me, Nate," I said.

Then the stick exploded. The fire blew apart as if some monster were erupting from the ground beneath the campfire. Flaming logs and showers of orange embers flew everywhere. We immediately crouched and covered our heads as some of the debris hit us. Nate had been right that we were too close at first.

A group of children came running from different parts of the cavern. I suddenly felt embarrassed.

"Everything's all right. I was only demonstrating to Annabelle what we use as our main source of explosives. No one is hurt. You can go back to what you were doing. Sorry for the scare. I promise that I'll yell out a warning if I ever do that again."

Nate was laughing as he helped me to my feet.

"What's so funny?" I asked.

"The look on your face was worth everyone getting mad at me. You didn't think anything would happen, did you?"

"Of course, I did. Where I come from, ordinary tree branches always explode," I said, with a degree of anger.

"Thanks, Nate. Now we have to rebuild the fire," Lizzy said as she and Kyle moved into the area again.

"Sorry. I'd help you guys, but I have a lot to show Annabelle," Nate said.

As we hurriedly moved away from the destroyed fire, I said, "Okay, so how exactly does a stick explode?"

"We first discovered the explosive possibilities of the trees years ago. A boy did just what you did. He was only building a fire when he tossed on a branch collected from a deeper part of the forest. A few of the kids were injured but not seriously hurt. As you guessed by now, we did name the trees. They're called Kablooey Trees. The trees turn charred black when they die. It almost looks as if they burned in a recent fire. There's a process happening in the wood as the tree dies. We've never been able to identify what's going on with this process. The living trees don't explode like that. The deadwood is highly reactive to heat and makes the entertaining display you've just seen. That small stick is only about a third of what we use in each of our explosive charges."

We approached the wall again. I watched the waves rush in, lap against the ship and across the port before losing momentum. I thought of another question and fired it off.

"How do you get the long pieces of lumber down here?" I was sure that I knew the answer, but I wanted to make sure Nate wasn't hiding another entrance to the cavern.

"You must have figured out that some of the collected lumber was too long to come down the well. The wood goes over the edge of the cliff. Several people go in the water, work the pieces under the wall into the cavern. There are only three people who are allowed to do this because of the danger. They're powerful swimmers and know how to handle the waves against the cliff wall. If they face serious trouble with the waves, all they have to do is go underwater and swim into the cavern. We removed more than thirty feet of the wall below the surface of the water. We made sure to make this deep enough, so we don't have any problems getting the ship out of here. I can't think of a worse situation than spending all this time building the ship, only to hang up on the part of the rock wall we never cleared away."

"That brings me to my next question. You told me before about bringing the wall down and sailing from the cavern and back to the gateway. How on earth are we going to get the ship from the cavern?" I asked.

"That's something I'd rather show than tell. Come on, let's go this way."

He led me along a path running toward the back of the cavern. Even with the torch Nate had, it was incredibly dark in this part of the cavern. I desperately tried to avoid stumbling over loose rocks but still managed a few painful falls. The ceiling was low enough that we had to crouch as we reached the back wall.

"Now, place your hand against the wall and tell me what you feel," he said.

I did and said, "Wet."

"Yes, good. More to the point, what you're feeling is some of the ocean water bleeding through the rock wall."

"How's that possible? We can't be on the other side of the island."

"No, we're not even close. What's actually on the other side of this thin wall is a sort of river. There's a void running from one end of the island to the other. This underground area is filled with ocean water constantly racing from one end of the island to the other," Nate told me.

I was suddenly getting the whole picture. I now understood how the Good Ship was going to set sail.

"You're going to blow this wall down as well, aren't you? You're going to let the force of the rushing water push the ship from the cavern, right?"

"Like a cork from a bottle under pressure. Maybe not that fast, but pretty fast. The water is going to funnel along the bottom of the cavern, running into our port. The water will hit the ship's stern with significant force and shove us through the newly-made opening in the wall. I can't say it's a perfect plan, but it's at least a decent one."

I was impressed with the planning in setting the ship to sail. However, everything that went on paper didn't necessarily mean the entire plan would go accordingly.

"I want to know more about the ship and exactly how this massive thing came to be," I said.

"Well, another major part of our operation is right over there. Without this area, there's no way the construction of the ship could have happened."

91

Nate led me to a section of the cavern that was the brightest and the hottest. Two boys worked beside a medium-sized pit carved out of the cavern floor. The pit had an intensely bright orange fire and a constant roll of smoke coming from it.

"This is our forging area. It's the place we're able to make such things as nails, steel bands, brackets, chains, cannonballs, all sorts of tools, and anything else we might need to put the ship together. Over the years, we've been able to take all kinds of metals from the sunken ships. Everything is melted down and shaped into whatever we need. Lead liquefies fairly easy, but steel takes a great deal more heat. We have to use fine shavings from a Kablooey Tree to ramp up the heat high enough. The fires get insanely hot when we crank them up to melt steel. There are several natural vent holes in the ceiling of the cavern that allows the heat and smoke to escape," Nate said.

"That's pretty cool," I said, stealing one of Nate's words.

"Yep. Look here," Nate said as he retrieved what looked to be two clay pots from a shelf and handed them to me.

"I didn't know you did pottery as well."

"Sort of, but we don't use these for eating or drinking. You have a whole cast when you place them together. This one is for making cannonballs. Do you see the small hole in the top? We bind the two pieces firmly together and pour liquefied steel into the top. When it cools, we've got a solid chunk of steel that fits perfectly into our cannons.

We walked back to the ship. I've so far learned a lot about their operation in less than an hour. I couldn't wait to get started on whatever Nate had in mind for today's activity. I wanted to become a full-fledged member of the team and learn all the crafts. It's time for me to pull my weight around here and earn my keep.

"So what's in the works for today? I don't think I'm quite ready to fool around with exploding sticks or melting metal just yet, but I'm up for nearly anything else," I said.

"Are you?" he asked with a grin.

"Be nice to me. I said nearly anything. I'm still a beginner, so remember that when you assign work detail."

"I'm always nice, even when I try not to be. I've got something in mind for you. How do you feel about heights and getting completely dirty?"

Twenty minutes later, I was dangling from the ship by a simple rope and board contraption. Nate volunteered me to coat the outside of the boat with a resin type that he called *gum*.

Gum, as it turned out, came from different types of trees spotted throughout the island. Nate told me that the compound resin bleeds from these trees and is collected daily. He explained that this stuff was heated to liquid form and then used as an incredibly durable glue and a protective shield for the hull when it cooled. During the early building stages, the area below the surface was treated when the ship was in dry-dock. After completing the ship's outside, they applied several heavy gum coats across the hull to protect the ship from leaking and the wood from rotting.

Nate loved nothing more than to make everything a hands-on deal for me. I spent over an hour brushing on another layer of the gum to a section of the starboard.

Nate leaned over the railing and said, "Are you just going to hang around all day, or are you going to work?"

"Comedian of the year right there," I announced to anyone within earshot.

"It's probably a good idea to get that stuff washed off your hands before it starts to harden. Otherwise, we'll have to use a hammer and chisel to break it free," Nate said and offered his all-famous smile.

"Crank me up. I'm ready for a break anyway. I think my legs fell asleep half an hour ago."

Nate and I grabbed a piece of fruit for a snack and then found a seat on the deck. It was almost a replay of the first time he brought me down here, except this time, I was a little wiser to the skills needed to make this particular society work.

"Thanks for everything today. I've had fun so far. The education has been enlightening," I said.

"By the end of the week, you'll be a professional at everything we do around here."

"I really can't see being a jack-of-all-trades, but I promise to give all of my assignments a solid one-hundred percent. You're a pretty good teacher when you're not doing your clowning around business," I said and then wrapped my arm around his shoulders.

"Clowning around is only a part-time job. I'm a lot better at making things happen."

I lightly rubbed my hand along the railing of the ship and said, "The time I've spent here is simply incredible. I'll never doubt the determination of a bunch of kids. I've never seen more intelligence or willingness to thrive before I came here. I can't imagine my time on this island getting more interesting or intense," I said.

"Well, you never know. This place has a way of fooling everyone. When you think things will begin to get boring, this island sometimes delivers wicked surprises," Nate said.

Sometimes Nate has an insight that would baffle the average person's mind. I should have known from the words of someone far wiser about the island's clockwork that my life was about to get incredibly hectic.

13

A Wandering Mistake

Our time below went by too fast. Before I knew it, our group had to rotate topside again. However, my education continued. There's simply no denying the fact that I wasn't very good at much, except finding myself in a mess of trouble. I tried to take Ella's advice and quickly learn the island's ways if I wanted to survive. Near the end of my third week on the island, I felt my best efforts slipping more and more. I was disappointed with myself, and, more importantly, I thought Nate was disappointed as well.

"Nate? Hey, Nate?" I said as I gently shook him from his late afternoon nap.

Nate's eyes opened and quickly focused on me. He was alarmed at first, but then after a quick look around, he must have guessed that nothing was wrong.

"What is it, Annabelle?"

I sat on the edge of the bed and said, "I'm going for a walk by myself."

Nate sat up, wiped the sleep from his eyes, and said, "I wouldn't recommend that. You don't know the woods very well. You don't know all of the different paths and where they lead. It's completely safe during the day if you stay on the right paths, but if you take a wrong turn, you could get into some serious trouble."

"Yeah, I know, but I just need to be alone for a while."

Nate has a knack for reading between the emotional lines when I desperately try to hide them.

"What's wrong?"

I closed my eyes and took a few deep breaths.

"I need time to be alone and think about things. I have bad dreams. It's been going on for the last couple of weeks. I've been dreaming a lot about my dad and brother. The dreams are so real that they always wake me up. I've had dreams of them in pain and dreams of them screaming," I said. Telling Nate this almost brought me to tears.

"I know. I've heard you talking in your sleep. I can't understand what you're saying, but I can tell you're having nightmares. You sometimes claw at the air as if you're battling an enemy. When the dreams have woken you, I've been acting like I'm asleep instead of comforting you as I should. These dreams of yours are something you need to overcome on your own. I want you to promise that you won't wander far."

"I won't," I promised.

I left the hut, went down the stairs, and headed toward the path leading to the well and the secret ship hiding within.

Nate poked his head out the window and called down to me. "Annabelle, wait!"

"I'll be back soon," I called over my shoulder.

"No, hang on. I want to give you something before you go. Just give me five minutes. Okay?"

"Time is irrelevant here, smarty pants! Whatever it is, hurry up."

After a short while, which I guessed to be more like ten minutes instead of five, Nate came stumbling down the stairs.

He ran over to me, gasping for breath.

"Here, take this just in case." He handed me a piece of paper. There were dozens of squiggly lines marking trails and horrible drawings indicating where base camp, the beach, the well, and other landmarks were. He had quickly drawn me a basic map of the island.

"It took you all that time to make this kindergartener sketch?" I teased.

"Can you believe I did all that from memory? Okay, so it's not perfect, but it will help."

"So, I'm going to take a wild guess and say that the big red X marks are not the location of buried treasure, but places I should avoid?"

"Right. Don't stay gone too long, or I'll have to send out a search party."

"Got it, boss," I said with a salute. I wasn't sure if he was joking about the search party.

One hundred yards down the trail, I turned to see the forest's thickness now completely obscured the base camp. I hadn't gone far, but now I was alone. Suddenly the idea didn't seem like such a good one. I pressed on as defiance to my fear and to see what lay at the ends of these trails.

I decided that it was best to use Nate's childish map to keep my bearings. I wanted to explore parts of the island I haven't yet seen. I was well aware of the dangers I could face if I had made the wrong choice in direction.

I've never denied that this island is one of the more beautiful places I've seen. Even if it lacked the magical things I've witnessed so far, I admit that it's something extra special. Maybe that's why there's a gateway created by some phenomenon that only allows access to those worthy enough. Just maybe.

A small group of birds followed me. Finch-sized birds were twittering at me in pleasant songs. They flew from tree to tree, keeping a steady pace with me. I rather enjoyed the extra company. I was happy they found me curious and felt the need to investigate. I welcomed them over the attention of the hunters, and that's no joke.

I couldn't say for sure how many paths had split off from the course I was on, but I took each one I saw. It was an immediate mistake, which left me in that uncomfortable place I like to call *lost*.

I studied the map. Dozens of lines twisted this way and that. It was difficult to remember if I had taken a right or left from the previous path. I hadn't seen any noticeable landmarks in quite some time.

"Okay, you can figure this out, Annabelle. Just look at where the sun is, which will help you get your bearings, and then use the map to backtrack to camp." I looked at the map again when I determined the sun's position.

After five minutes of looking at the map and turning it in my hands, I groaned with frustration, folded it, and stuck it in my back pocket. I'd decided the map was no more use, and I had no option except to continue forward until I came upon something I recognized.

"A little help here, please?" I asked the birds following my misguided quest.

They fluttered their wings and cocked their heads to watch me.

"Thanks, anyway."

I wasn't sure how many hours I've been walking, but I was noticing a series of cramps running through both of my calf muscles. I also noticed that my throat was as rough as sandpaper, and I hadn't the frame of mind to take a bottle of water with me. The only thing I had taken was a crudely drawn map that was rapidly leading me nowhere.

I approached an incline, which I was sure I hadn't come down. The path ran into darkness surrounded by dense trees and ivy tightly grown together. I couldn't even see through the crisscross weaving of the branches and leaves. I had a brief thought about turning back, but the curious side of me took control, and I pressed forward. There was a designed doorway as if the branches were grown this way on purpose. The only thing needed would be a hinged door, and the place was a naturally constructed castle wall. I looked left and right. The massive wall of trees extended as far as I could see in both directions.

At first, I didn't consider any menace hiding inside. The smarter thing to do was to turn back down the path. Just as I started to listen to the voice of caution, I saw a flash of brilliant blue. As I stepped closer to the doorway, the blue light multiplied. It was like watching the flashing of cameras taken by a bleacher-packed stadium. It was an incredible sight. I felt the unfortunate circumstances of the day temporarily lift from my heart.

"Hello?" I called out.

There was something about the flashing blue lights that calmed my nerves and made the experience seem harmless. These lights briefly reminded me of the lights displayed to me during my deep-sea dive weeks before. I never thought the lights in this place would attempt to trick me. I was seriously wrong.

When I stepped into that realm of beautiful swirling blue lights, the branches behind me began to change formation rapidly. The doorway there only a moment before was now closing as the creaking branches stretched and wove together. After only a minute, the entrance no longer existed. The blue lights then extinguished and left me in the blackness.

I had a horrifying thought that this place had a big red X on my map.

I heard something large glide through the trees above me. It moved stealthily as if the darkness didn't impair its navigation.

"Who's there?" I asked in a slightly trembling voice.

"We are all-knowing. We are of strength. We are of wisdom," the voice was deep and had a noticeable hiss to it.

"Show yourself," I said as I tried to remain calm.

"As you wish, Annabelle."

"How did you know my name?"

The blue lights I had seen a minute before now reappeared high in the trees. The light was bright enough to flood the area and allowed a small part of the fear to leave me. I couldn't immediately see the thing that had spoken, but I knew it was close.

"Where are you? What do you want from me?" I said.

"Want? I believe it was you who sought me out. Was it not?" The voice was still somewhere in the trees.

"I got lost in the woods. I'm just trying to find my way back. I saw the lights, and I got curious about what they were."

"Ah, those, my child, would be what you'd call bait. Creatures cannot resist my lights as those who enter here will never leave the same."

I tried to find the bravery within. If this unseen thing wanted a fight, then I wasn't going down without getting in a few swift punches.

"You didn't answer my questions. How did you know my name? And where are you?" I said.

"I answered the first question before you asked it. We are all-knowing. I can read your thoughts Annabelle Cross, daughter of John Cross and sister to Bradley. Sometimes Brad the Brat. Yes, I like that. I suppose to some people it's considered humorous. As for where I am, wherever I choose, my dear."

A powdery black mass trickled from the treetops like a falling cloud. It curled and parted on both sides of the outstretched branches. It was like a dozen fingers going separate ways and then combining as it reached the forest ground. The blackness swirled and elongated around the trunk of the nearest tree. The thing then began taking on a physical shape.

Green eyes ignited as the head took final shape. Its body finished shifting a moment later. What was staring at me was a massive black snake with glowing blue ripples firing down each side of its body in pulsing lightning bolt stripes.

"Not what you were expecting, I think," it hissed.

14

Serpents, Stones & Broken Bones

I tried to build my courage the best I could. I was making a stand against this thing now confining me. I took a step forward to prove my lack of fear.

"Easy now, brave one," the serpent spoke.

I noticed that the voice no longer came from the creature but instead seemed to come from everywhere as if it were an echo.

"Not an echo, child. I'm here inside your head."

The serpent was reading my mind. It invaded my private thoughts as I could feel something moving around inside my brain, something probing. I pinched my eyes shut. I no longer saw the green fire of its eyes. Just as quickly, I felt the squirming probes in my mind vanish.

"You're smarter than most. The other children I've trapped so far never understood that a person's eyes are open doorways to the mind. You shouldn't believe that keeping your eyes closed will protect you from what I want," the creature hissed. The voice was no longer in my head but now heard aloud.

"And what is it you want from me?"

"To do the same as what I do to all those who I capture. I want to drain all the goodness from you. It's the first step taken to prepare you for a long life of misery.

When I'm through with you, happiness won't even be a distant memory. All you will know from this day forward will be an unquenchable thirst for hate and greed. Only then will you be ready for recruitment into the Army."

"The Jade Army?"

"Is there another kind?"

Of course, I thought, and I sure could have used them right now with their guns blazing and grenades exploding.

Something curled around my ankles. I kept my eyes closed tight but tried to kick away whatever it was. It wasn't just one thing but dozens of slithering bodies wrapping around me.

"Are the hunters also under your control? When they take a child from the forest, do they bring them back to you?" I said.

"Little naïve Annabelle. You need to open your ears and your mind. I told you when you first stepped into my domain. *We are all-knowing.* They are me, and I am them. We are one."

I let my right eye open slightly. I looked down, trying to get an idea of what kind of things were on me. I regretted looking. What moved at my feet were more snakes. Before I snapped my eye shut again, I saw a small cluster of fist-sized stones just beyond the squiggling mass at my feet.

I couldn't help it. The sight of those curling, slimy snakes circling my feet made me release a shrill scream.

"Annabelle?" I heard a distant voice call out.

Who was that? I knew it hadn't been the voice of the creature. It was a voice that was good and caring. I was sure it was Nate's voice.

"Nate, Nate, I'm here!" I called at the top of my voice.

"Yes, yes, invite them in, more happy memories to steal. Your little savior has come for you, Annabelle. No, wait, there's more than one. Yes, many friends have come searching for you."

"Where, Annabelle?" Nate's muffled voice asked.

"Behind the wall of trees. Hurry!"

"Cut the branches!" I heard Nate call out to the others who had joined him in the search.

"Oh, how wonderful. I could easily let your friends in, but I do enjoy this sort of fun. Let's see what methods they choose to take when I do this," the serpent said.

"It's not working. The branches are growing back!" another voice frantically said.

There's one notable thing about myself I'd like to mention here. Although I'm a girl, I certainly don't throw like one. I can rocket a ball at the speeds of professional baseball pitchers. I also have the accuracy to match. My father proudly said it's a fluke of nature and that I should use this gift at every possible chance.

I took his advice now. I rapidly shuffled my feet to work the tightening knot of snakes from my legs. I made brief eye contact with the serpent's deep glowing green eyes as I leaped free from the tangle of black snakes. I landed beside the cluster of stones I had spotted a moment before. I grabbed one in each hand. I calculated the stone's weight with lightning mental speed, the distance to my target, and the trajectory needed for a precise strike. I cocked my right arm back and threw the stone with every bit of strength I had.

Although the serpent had cascaded down from the trees minutes ago in a cloudlike roll, it was now a physical creation. The stone zipped beneath those blue lights and found its mark. The stone connected brilliantly between the fires of the serpent's eyes. Its head pulled back, and its entire body reacted to the strike, making the tree tremble. I was sure the hit had possibly hurt the giant creature. It looked around as if confused about what had happened.

Please hurry, Nate, I thought.

I transferred the other stone to my right hand and moved behind a large tree. I tried to figure out my next move. The problem was I couldn't think of one.

I heard movement. I peeked around the trunk of the tree and saw that the serpent was gone. My eyes searched the forest grounds and found nothing. I started scanning the treetops from where the thing originally appeared.

I spotted a bright glow to my left. I turned and cocked my arm back for another fastball. The light I saw wasn't something caused by the serpent but was instead fire on the wall of branches from which I had entered this place. The fire quickly spread.

I couldn't figure out what was going on for a brief moment, and then I understood. My friends on the other side gave up trying to cut the branches away. Instead, they set fire to the seemingly impenetrable barrier.

The branches hastily retreated from the blaze, and the doorway reopened. A small group of children broke through. Some had torches in hand, while others held drawn bows, clubs, or knives. If I hadn't been so terrified, I might have laughed at the sight. They looked like eighteenth-century townsmen prepared to capture a witch and burn her.

I ran to them.

"We need to leave quickly," Nate said.

"I couldn't agree more," I said as we slowly backed through the burning hole.

The blue lights above blinked out. Now there was only the fire of the torches and the expanding crackling flames in the wall of branches.

"Everyone run!" Nate shouted.

No one had a problem following the order. The group of children sprinted back down the path and toward the safety of the base camp.

What happened next was a nightmare, somehow pulling its way into reality.

The air around us was pulled into the realm of the serpent as if something larger than life took a deep breath. What exhaled from that place was an explosion of black figures through the roaring flames. It was as I had first witnessed the serpent. It wasn't something whole, but a dozen reaching lengths of tentacles shot through the fire with enough force that burning branches and orange embers flew by us.

The individual serpent shapes began transforming mid-air. I glanced back several times simply because the astonishing sight was one I couldn't ignore. As the things hit the ground and raced behind us, I could see the arching of spines, the growth of legs, tails, and heads. Finishing the transformation was the igniting blaze of cold blue eyes.

The hunters are coming.

Nighttime is here, and there was no stopping them.

I wasn't sure how far we were from base camp. I was positive that it was far enough we wouldn't get there before being snatched in the jaws of the black shadows following close behind.

When I chanced another look, I saw one of the black figures at Aidan's heels. A horrified expression came to his face as the thing seized his legs and brought him down. Within only seconds, the thing pulled back into the darkness of the night and dragged Aidan with it.

Nate also witnessed this. He must have thought we'd have a better chance in small numbers because he yelled out for everyone to split up.

Nate, Max, and I quickly parted from the others as we took a sharp left. Several pairs of blue eyes raced behind us.

"What's the plan?" I asked, out of breath.

"Run faster," Max said.

I heard the pounding of the hunters right behind us. I knew that any second, they would leap and take the three of us down. Max must have figured the same defeat. A second later, he was abruptly stopping and swung his torch at one of the approaching hunters. The flaming end crushed against the creature's head, and immediately the hunter became a ball of fire. I was amazed that something that was nothing more than a black cloud a minute ago was now on fire. The hunter ran in tight circles while snapping its jaws at the flames, engulfing its entire body.

As Max swung the torch to keep the other hunters at bay, I felt something scurry around my feet. When I looked down, I saw hundreds of tiny bodies running through the undergrowth. In the dark, I couldn't immediately tell what they were. When I heard the familiar barking of their voices, I realized what was moving in the night. A platoon of mischief propelled themselves into the air and onto the backsides of the hunters. The small fairy-like creatures joined the fight.

The hunters turned in panic and began clamping the mischief in their powerful jaws. There were far too many for the hunters to have a chance. I saw squads of fairies sinking small knives, teeth, and claws into the bodies of the hunters. One mischief rapidly climbed one of the hunter's backs and across its neck. The little thing then gripped a black ear, sank its sharp teeth, and shook its head until the ear came apart in a wisp of smoke.

I heard a loud groaning next as if a giant were suddenly and rudely awoken. As two of the hunters lunged for us, I saw something much larger than them moving through the night. Thick tree branches were sweeping across the forest ground. Nate, Max, and I rolled out of the way. The fairies also gave up their battle and fled in a wave as the branches caught the two hunters on a collision course. The two dark figures launched into the night sky. As I stare disbelievingly, the hunters spun apart in a black mist taken away in the night breeze.

The forest was now alive with the sweeping motion of grouch trees. They were making a steady attack on all of the hunters pursuing the small groups of children. The large branches came crashing down on the bodies and glowing eyes of those relentless stalkers. Instead of being crushed and battered into pulp, the hunters burst apart in a puff of black smoke.

A kid in the distance suddenly went down and disappeared in the thick forest growth. Two more kids went down, vanishing as the trees continued the assault on the retreating hunters. The trees were able to save four other children from being dragged away.

I smelled something horrid. It was almost like burnt hair, only not quite the same. I realized what it was seconds too late.

"That was close. Why would the mischief and grouch trees help us?" Max asked.

"There's something—" I didn't have time to finish.

The something I was speaking about was the charred hunter that was on fire a minute ago but somehow managed to put itself out. The foliage at Max's back came alive with movement. Max quickly went down as something grabbed him, and the terrified screams were all that remained as the hunter dragged him into darkness.

Tree branches came smashing down, but all had missed the fleeing hunter.

"Max!" Nate and I screamed.

All we could see was the trailing flames of the torch Max still held. We ran the freshly made path only to reach the torch and nothing else. Max was gone.

"No, no, no," Nate said as he picked up the torch and spun around.

Our constant calling attracted the rest of the children who had come to save my life. Max wasn't one of them. I noticed that at least half a dozen other faces were missing. All of the children remaining were battered, broken, and exhausted from the fight.

I placed my hand on Nate's shoulder as his eyes searched the darkness. I felt my heartbreak when he glanced at me with a look of hatred, and then he angrily brushed my hand away.

"I'm so sorry, Nate. I'm sorry for everything," I said.

"Yeah, I'm sorry that we came for you," he said.

No words in my thirteen years of life have ever stung so deeply.

"We can't stand here. We need to get back to camp. There's nothing we can do for the others. They're gone, and I don't think anyone is coming back from that place," Remy said as he turned and closely watched the night.

"Someone needs to help me. I think I have a broken ankle," Anthony said as he hopped closer to us.

"My wrist might have broken when one of the tree branches came down," Shane said while cradling his injured arm.

"Let's go," Nate said somberly and led us home.

15

Eight for One

Morale was a faded memory when our group finally reached base camp and took refuge in the treetops. There hadn't been any more hunters in pursuit on our travel back, so our numbers didn't decline anymore. Remy had glumly counted heads as we ran toward home. Eight were missing from the group, three girls and five boys. All of the children have done the bravest action I've ever seen. They faced possible death to save one of their own.

The problem is simple; I didn't feel like one of the team. I feel like an outcast accepted out of pity. I feel like the children took me in because I had nowhere else to go. Truthfully, I felt like a disease rotting away this tightly knit group from the inside. I wanted to shrink away into the night and pretend like I didn't exist.

Some of the injured children were led back to one of the huts. Some of them had sustained lacerations, and two of them had suffered broken bones. Naomi tended to them to the best of her abilities. She said they would need to make a wrist and leg cast out of cloth and resin in the morning.

As everyone retired to their rooms, I wasn't surprised when Nate told me it wasn't the best of ideas that I share a room with him tonight. When I backed out of the hut with my head hung in shame, I heard him start to cry.

I also started quietly crying when I was alone. I sat in the middle of one of the bridges. My legs were dangling over the edge, and my arms wrapped around the suspension ropes. I briefly hoped that the bridge supports would give out, and I would plummet to my death. I thought just maybe that would be better for everyone.

Max had endured seven long years riddled with a bad case of the flu that wouldn't ease up. He battled his way through only to be kidnapped a short while later and now facing a terror far worse than a venomous beetle bite.

I heard someone approaching from one of the walkways. The bridge slightly bounced under the movement as Jasmine sat beside me. She was one of the elders who had stayed behind with the younger children as the others came for me.

"I hope you're not planning on jumping because then we'd have to dig a grave tomorrow, and that would be even more work-work-work," she said.

"You should leave me down there and let the scavengers gnaw away at me. Then you can toss the bones into the woods. Problem solved."

"You're pretty hard on yourself, Annabelle. You didn't ask for them to come after you."

"Nope, I sure didn't. But it was my carelessness that caused eight good people to be taken away to who knows where. Do you have someone who the hunters or the Jade Army has taken?" I asked.

"Everyone you've met has a father, mother, brother, or sister on the other side. We've always believed in being rejoined with those lost to the darkness of the Jade Army."

"I keep asking Nate about his family, but he always puts off the conversation. I think talking about them scares him," I said.

"I imagine so. I sure wouldn't want to face the hatred of the Jade King. Family matters like that can be a hard thing to deal with," Jasmine said.

I turned to her. In the pale moonlight, her face seemed burdened with years of building hope and then crushing back down. She was one of many who battled the torments of time on this island.

"What do you mean by family matters?"

Jasmine turned and smiled. "He didn't tell you, did he?"

"Tell me what?"

"I don't suppose it's my place to say, but what the heck. I can't imagine temperaments getting any worse around here. I'm not at all saying that this unbinding is your fault. It always happens when we rotate topside that ambition seems to diminish within all of us. We always want to be working on the Good Ship. The ship is the glue binding us all. Being up here is also necessary. We have to dive and collect anything we can from the wreckage of the ships. We have to tend gardens. We have to scout the beaches for more people who come through the gateway."

"I see how everyone has a part to play. I think mine is finding my way directly into trouble," I said.

"We've all had our share of struggles on this island. Anyway, you went face-to-face with Simora and survived to tell the tale. Congratulations."

I quickly placed the name. The wheels of time turned back weeks to my first day on the island. Nate had taken me to the waterfall and shared an exciting story of the twin sisters, Lothlora and Simora. According to Nate's story, they were the creators of these lands and all dwelling creatures. Their different points of view became so great that a battle had ensued, and the power making them whole fractured. Simora was the greedy, controlling sister wishing to show her dominance over all of the creatures.

"You walked right into her domain and bravely fought her until the others came for you. Some children haven't so lucky. Nate and his family were shipwrecked sometime at the beginning of the century. Max, Nate, and Nate's twin brother, Roland, made it to the island. I can tell you that Roland was always a hot-tempered kid. Like most kids, he didn't follow guidance very well. Instead, Roland defied everything he was supposed to do. I suppose you could say that he was a kid set in his ways. One day he set out with twelve others on a scouting mission. Just like you, they wandered right into Simora's domain. It was Simora who infected Roland and the others with a growing seed of hate and greed. When the group returned, they told us they were leaving to build a camp of their own. Thirteen of them walked into the woods and never came back. It's believed that they moved to the island north of this one. It's only a guess because we've never found them on this island. I'm sure those thirteen boys found others who Simora has infected. It's a popular belief that Roland became the controlling force behind the army. That's why I called him the Jade King earlier," Jasmine said.

"Where are all the parents now?" I said.

"Taken. It wasn't long after the boys left when the hunters first arrived at our camp on the beach and began snatching the strongest and smartest members of our group. The adults were the first ones to be taken. Night after night, the hunters came back and stole the fittest people from our group. I think we're glad that we weren't bright enough or strong enough to be one of the selected. They took the best of us so that their army would be undefeatable when the time of war comes around. At least that's the theory."

"So then you built these huts in the trees to protect yourselves from the hunters coming back for more of you?" I said.

"Right. During the day, we worked in the trees, constructing buildings and bridges as our refuge. We slept uncomfortably on small platforms and in the crook of tree branches for months before we finally had a proper place to call home."

"What exactly is Simora?"

Jasmine shrugged. "Who can say for sure? She's an evil presence who has been here far longer than we have. So far as we know, you're the only one at this camp who has faced her and walked away from it. I imagine everyone will be suspicious of you from this point on. Most kids will suspect that whatever awful thing she's done to the other children was done to you. They'll probably treat you like a spy or something from now on. The Jade Army has sent spies here before. Most of them were easy to detect because they seem void of all human emotions other than hate. We always send them away unharmed, but we tell them if they ever return, they'll face possible death."

"When I was in that place, and she made eye contact with me, it was like she was pulling out every decent part of me. If the others hadn't come for me, there's no way I would have escaped," I said.

"Let's just hope for your sake she left something good behind," Jasmine said, now studying me with a degree of suspicion.

"It was only a few seconds before I was able to break eye contact with Simora. Don't worry about me. I still feel all the things I felt before. Right now, I'm just feeling stupid and a great disappointment to everyone."

Jasmine lightly punched me in the shoulder and said, "Hey, maybe the other eight kids were sacrificed because it'll be up to you to turn the tables in our favor when this battle comes face-to-face, and it will certainly come face-to-face. It would help if you kept that in mind. It might help you get through the events that happened earlier."

"It's hard to believe something like that, but I'll try to see it that way. Thanks, Jasmine."

"Don't mention it. I'm going to bed. There's a place to sleep in my room if you don't have anywhere else to go."

"Thanks again. I'll probably have to do that. I'm just going to stay out here for a little while longer," I said, offering a weak smile.

"Okay. Goodnight, Annabelle."

"Goodnight."

Many bad things have come around in my life, but being stranded on this island wasn't one of them. I've been waiting a long time for something epic to happen. I've waited for anything to come along and take away the monotony of everyday life on the water.

I thought about everything Jasmine told me. I tried to build hope and faith, but I didn't feel like I had any purpose at all. I sat on the bridge for half the night, staring into the darkness and thinking about what I was going to do. My eyes could barely stay open when an idea struck me. I have to leave camp. I have to find the main base of the Jade Army. I have to take back what was recently stolen.

16

A Journey in the Wild

The world has a different perspective just before the sun. There's a certain stillness about the predawn on this island. It's a brief moment when the nocturnal prowlers finish their activities of searching for food and seek shelter. The animals that hunt by daylight are awakening during this time, and in turn, these different creatures pass each other by routine.

There's a moment when the sun's rays first break the horizon and bring a peaceful calm to the land. During this time of the day's birth, I chose to set out into the unknown.

I wouldn't exactly say I had a plan. I wouldn't exactly say I had even a vague idea of where I was going or what I would do once I got there. I also wouldn't exactly say I believed beyond the shadow of a doubt that I could accomplish the task of infiltrating the Jade Army's camp and take back those abducted last night.

Although there are many unanswered questions, I was going to surge forward. I desperately wanted to find and free my friends.

Truthfully, I knew I was running away from those who are now wishing me away from this place. I've let each of them down over the short time I've been here. I was thinking maybe my attempt or success at retrieving the abducted eight would somehow reconstruct the damages I've caused so far. All I knew for sure was that I couldn't face the group today. The guilt of my idiotic actions was eating me alive.

I quietly slipped from my bedding on the floor, collected my pack, and left Jasmine's hut. I had managed only a few hours of restless sleep. My muscles ached, and my mind was fuzzy from lack of rest. I silently made my way to one of the ropes used as a quick escape from the treetops. I didn't want to risk lowering the stairs and waking the group. I just wanted to be history when everyone rolled out of bed.

The warming rays of the sun began touching the forest when my feet hit the ground. The hunters would be hiding in Simora's domain until nightfall. I hoped that would give me sufficient time to get to wherever I was going.

I knew from Jasmine's conversation last night that the north island is said to be the home of the Jade Army. I had to move quickly. If the journey took too long, then I'd need to find a place to fortify myself for the night before the hunters came out again.

I made sure this time to be prepared for my quest into the wilderness. I had packed extra clothing, a pocketknife, matches, some fruit, and sufficient water. It's a lesson learned from my misguided wandering that yesterday led me into the realm of the speaking serpent.

Exactly how far away the next island is has remained a mystery to me. If it were close enough, I could swim it with little trouble. If the distance were too great, then my journey to the northern shore would be for nothing.

I found a path running directly north. I tried following the dividing paths continuing in that direction. Some of the courses led to a completely different heading. Several times I had to backtrack to a previous route.

I heard a scurry of movement in the weeds to my left, immediately stopping me. I retrieved the knife from my pocket and unfolded the blade. My preparation for the worst to come was short-lived. Two martens bounced from the tangle of weeds, leaped onto the trunk of a nearby tree, and proceeded to chase each other in play.

I slowly walked to the tree. The martens paused their game long enough to study my approach. They didn't flee when I stepped within a few feet of them.

"Hello there. My name is Annabelle. What are your names?" I said.

The marten on the lower part of the trunk quickly climbed the bark to the side of its friend. Their oil drop eyes watched me. Neither of them answered.

"No need to be shy. I won't hurt you. Can you tell me whether or not I'm heading in the right direction to reach the northern shore?"

"What are you doing?" a voice behind me asked.

I whirled around to discover that Graur was standing on the path. He watched me with an amused interest, as did the martens. I realized I was the center of attention.

"Oh, I didn't know you were there, Graur. You startled me. I was asking these martens for the right way to the northern shore."

"Asking the martens, were you? Ha. You would be standing here for quite some time before they gave you a logical answer. To tell you plainly, they're martens, Annabelle. They have no vocal cords that can produce human speech. I'd also like to add that they certainly don't have the mental wit to understand your words," Graur said.

"Oh," I said, suddenly feeling like a complete fool.

"That's all right. You were probably under the assumption that all animals here can communicate with you. A few others and I are an exception. I've lived for a very long time, and I have learned much. I assure you that learning the tongue of man was no easy task but a rewarding challenge. Tell me, why do you seek the northern shore?"

"There's just something I must do," I said, as I focused on the dirt at my feet.

"I see. Well, yes, you are still on the correct heading. I should inform you that you'll only find wickedness in that direction. You would be wise to return to your camp."

"I can't go back there until I do this one thing. Maybe then I can return with the burden of guilt lifted," I said.

"Yes, I understand. Word travels fast among the animals of the island. I heard of the unfortunate conflict last night that the hunters took several members of your group."

"Eight of them," I told him.

"I fail to see how surrendering to the Jade Army will remove the guilt resting on your heart. What you're on is a pointless mission."

"I wasn't going to hand myself over to the Jade Army. I was going to get my friends back."

Graur's head lowered and slowly shook side to side. "Once taken, there's no coming back, Annabelle. You shouldn't have any delusions about that. I've never witnessed the return of someone from the Jade Army coming back to your group. Once Simora has stripped the kindness from one's heart, they never return."

"You're wrong," I shouted. My words echoed off the thick surroundings of the forest.

"They're gone, Annabelle," Graur said patiently.

120

"The others are not yet beyond our reach. Not my friends, and not my father and brother. I can get them all back," I said defiantly.

Graur's head raised. Our eyes connected. I'm not sure if it was my undying need to get them back, or maybe it was the belief that I possibly had the means to do as I claimed. In any case, Graur's tail wagged, and his face suddenly brightened.

"Then I shall join you, Annabelle. Your quest is now our quest," Graur said and stepped to my side.

"I honestly don't want to place you in harm's way, but I sure would enjoy the company, especially if it's one who knows the island."

"Well, your choice of guides is limited at this point. I know the island well, and I should think that I can hold my own if conflict finds us," Graur said. His florescent green eyes were wise and full of strength.

"I never doubted it for a second. I always knew you had the courageous heart of a lion," I teased and patted Graur's head.

"Uh, please, Annabelle, to pat my head is belittling my advanced intelligence. I'm not your ordinary mutt that does tricks for treats."

"Oh, I didn't mean anything by doing that. I'm sorry."

"Now I'm the one teasing," Graur said and nuzzled my dangling hand.

I smiled, stroked his head, and scratched behind his ears. His eyes closed, and his head rolled tighter into my palm. I let out a laugh as Graur's right hind leg lifted and began rapidly kicking in the air as my fingers found the magical nerves affecting this far-reaching area of his body.

"It's been some time since I've allowed anyone to do that. Oh, how I've missed it!"

121

"Well, just let me know if the need is there again. I have ten willing fingers," I said as we traveled down the narrow path.

"Nate told me that it was your father and brother who the Jade Army had taken when you arrived here."

"Yeah. The Jade Army blew our boat apart. As the boat was sinking, something hit me over the head, and I blacked out. When I came around, I thought they had drowned. Nate assures me that they didn't go down with the boat. He said the Jade Army wouldn't allow the sea to take potential slaves. I believe him. I believe they're on the northern island," I said.

I realized it was becoming more difficult each time I spoke about my father and Brad. I've started thinking of them as I did my mother. They were becoming memories as if my mind already accepted them dead and never to be seen again. It was easier for my mind to picture them as deceased instead of the thought of them being alive, only turned into an unthinkable and hateful shell of their former selves.

"When you encountered Simora, in what form did she appear?" Graur asked.

"A large black serpent. Why? Does she show herself in different ways?"

"I couldn't say for sure. Simora is an ancient evil. Her powers can see into the deepest reaches of your mind and find what you fear most. The hunters, as you call them, are all small pieces of her existence. They're powerful and able to change shape with ease when they are close to her domain. I believe that when the hunters leave Simora's domain, they become a physical creation. I don't know this for sure, but this theory would explain why they cannot change shapes and climb the trees after you. I also believe that the farther away they are from her, the weaker and less frightening they become," Graur said.

"Somehow, I doubt that last part. I think I'd be terrified no matter how far away we were from Simora's nest. For some reason, the grouch trees and the mischief helped us last night. The trees smashed their branches on them. The hunters blew apart in a puff of black smoke. Does that mean we destroyed those hunters? Does it mean that we also destroyed a part of Simora?"

Graur halted. I stopped and turned to face him.

"Do you see those yellow flowers to your left? Those are called liliqeets. They are very delicious and nutritious for your species. Break them off at the stem and put them in your pack for later."

I did as he suggested.

"Simora was once a powerful entity that dominated all of the lands. As a thousand years go by, even the strongest and wisest of beings become weaker. The only thing giving her power these days is what she takes from each of you. That's why she has become relentless at trying to capture all of those found without protection. She steals a part of each person, which mostly replenishes her power used during the chase. I don't think she's able to catch enough of you to replenish all of the energy she's lost over the centuries."

"So if her power is fading over time, and the children are finally free from this island, does that mean that Simora will eventually vanish from existence?"

"I suspect it would take a great deal of time to pass, but, yes, Simora would no longer be a dominating force," Graur said.

"I hope so. Good riddance to serpent rubbish." I looked at Graur and smiled.

The corners of his mouth slightly curled up, and his tail swished at the thought.

"If I'm not mistaken, that was a smile, and a good one at that," I said and then laughed. I reached out and scratched behind Graur's ears again. Having him following me on this strange quest was a welcoming relief.

"I'd love nothing more than to see Simora fade to nothingness, and the animals of these islands live in freedom once again," Graur said.

"I'd love to see that as well. As for me, I'd like to go to the place I call home. After everything we've experienced since our travels through the gateway, I'm willing to bet that my father would be more eager to settle down. Maybe we'll even find a nice house somewhere beautiful. Maybe my father might even consider remarrying. I'm not sure if my brother and I are ready to accept a new mother, but I think that it would make my father very happy."

"I wish I had words of wisdom I could preach to you on this subject," Graur said.

I removed the pack from my shoulders, knelt, and unzipped one of the pockets. I took a long drink of water. I decided to be brave and sample a taste of the flower Graur had me pick. I pulled off a petal and popped it into my mouth. My taste buds quickly exploded with delight.

"I can't believe it! It tastes just like buttered popcorn!"

17

A Place Called Unhappiness

Less than a half-hour later, Graur and I reached the northern shore without incident. There were no beaches here. Instead, the forest grew right up to the waterline. The trail we were following ran directly into the water.

"Does that seem a little strange to you, Graur? This path seems well used. I'm sure that no one from our camp comes up this way. At least I've never heard of anyone traveling to the northern shore," I said.

I looked up from the trail. My eyes searched the rippling blue water. I saw what I needed to find. Nearly three miles from my feet was the rugged shore of another island. The island protruded from the water like the jagged green tooth of a mammoth ocean monster.

Graur lowered his head and began sniffing the path and investigating my suspicion of others continuously using the trail.

"There's no way I can swim that. If it were half the distance, then maybe I could. I can't swim that far in the battling waves. I wouldn't have a chance. I'd probably cramp up and drowned halfway out there," I said, as the grim realization struck my mind.

"Swim? I don't believe there will be a need for that, Annabelle," Graur said. His highly tuned sense of smell took him to overgrown ivy covering an area on the left side of the path.

I stepped beside him, grabbed a handful of the vines, and pulled it to the side. Beneath the strands of ivy was a roughly built canoe. The canoe contained only two oars and nothing else. The ivy had begun to turn a light shade of brown. I noticed there weren't any roots from this plant. Someone has recently transplanted the ivy to cover up the canoe.

"Why is someone trying to hide this canoe?" I asked.

"More importantly, *who* is taking this canoe to the other island?" Graur said.

My mind started moving at high speeds.

"Someone from the Jade Army is on the island. They must have sent a spy," I said.

"Look at these footprints and canoe tracks in the mud. They're leading out to sea. That means there are more than one canoe and more than one person."

"Maybe that means several people met here, exchanged information, and parted ways. One headed back to camp while the other paddled to the island to share the information with the Jade Army," I suggested.

"I believe you're right, Annabelle. There's perhaps a spy among your group of friends."

"If that's true, then it means the Jade Army knows about the Good Ship. They know that it's nearly complete and, more importantly, its location," I said as I studied the distant island.

"We should turn back and deliver the news to your friends. They need to know right away that a member of your group is untrustworthy. They need to find out the information this person has recently shared."

I thought about that. Us going back to camp and telling others about our discovery was an obvious move.

I did still feel a reluctance about going back without the missing eight. I felt Nate had placed a degree of resentment on me. I had to at least come back with Max to make things right between us.

"We will, but not right now. I have to go to the other island and see the kind of evil we're facing. I have to try to get some of my friends back."

I grabbed one end of the canoe and pulled it free from its hiding place. I maneuvered it along the path and into the water. I threw my pack in and then hopped into the canoe. I looked back at Graur. His eyes showed a hint of indecision as if this were the last time we would speak.

"Hopefully, I'll be back in a few hours. If everything goes according to my strange plan, that is. If you happen to run into anyone from our group, will you tell them to be on the lookout for a spy?"

"I'd like to do that for you, Annabelle, but I'm afraid I'm busy elsewhere," Graur said and leaped from the shore into the small canoe.

The boat shifted, nearly overturned, but then righted itself without either of us going in the water. I wanted to protest Graur's voluntary action to follow me into the lion's den, but again I was glad to have the company. I thought that just maybe he would come in handy should things turn ugly, and I needed help against fighting an entire army.

"Good. Since you're coming along, would you mind helping me paddle?" I said as I held out an oar.

Graur saw the smirk on my face and said, "That's one of the many reasons I like you, Annabelle. Even in a dire situation like this, you can find something witty and humorous to say."

I chuckled to myself as I paddled us to the distant island. The scenery was incredible. The magnificent view of the surrounding brilliant blue water and the mysterious islands spotting the horizon to my left was something extraordinary I didn't appreciate until now.

"I didn't know all these islands were out here. From our beach, near the campsite, you can't see any islands. How many are there?" I asked.

"No one knows for sure, except maybe Simora. All of the islands were once combined and under the control of Simora and her twin sister Lothlora. When their power was divided, everything fractured and hasn't been the same since. Now Simora's power barely reaches from one coast to the other on our island. I suppose the Jade Army has dominated the other islands if there's anything on them to overtake. To my knowledge, the Jade Army primarily dwells on the island in front of us. We know they only have a single ship. At least we've only seen one. It wouldn't surprise me if they were in the process of building another. As you can see, finding the materials and taking the time to build such a massive ship takes many years, even for a group as large as the Jade Army."

"So that's why our group has taken so long to build the Good Ship because the number of people the Jade Army has is far greater," I said.

Something suddenly hit the bottom of the canoe. I quickly pulled the oar from the water and carefully peered over the edge. Something long and orange darted beneath us. It was only a foot or two below the surface of the water, but it moved fast in its hit and run. I could have been wrong, but the thing resembled the creature I had seen while diving among the shipwrecks weeks before. It moved like soft rubber through the water. The entire thing looked as if it didn't have a single bone in its body. I could have sworn I saw a cluster of tentacles.

I remembered the book *20,000 Leagues Under the Sea*. During their adventure, a giant squid attacks Captain Nemo's submarine and nearly caused the entire crew's death.

"What was that?" I asked. My jumbled nerves caused my voice to crack.

"I couldn't say for sure. It certainly didn't seem friendly, whatever it was. I might have forgotten to mention earlier that I'm not a very strong swimmer. If the canoe overturns, I'll have to rely on you to rescue me and get us to the island," Graur said.

"And here I thought I was the only one with a sense of humor. I think that thing is gone now. Maybe it was just investigating us to see if we were edible. Hopefully, it realizes that a kid with little meat on her bones and a thing covered in hair wouldn't taste very good," I said as I continued to paddle.

"A thing covered in hair?" Graur said with resentment.

I smiled and kept my mouth shut.

A short while later, our canoe found land again. We were now in strange and dangerous territory. I kept my eyes wide and expected a clan to spring from the bushes in expectation of our arrival. I pulled the canoe onto a path I spotted a short distance from shore. It didn't take long before I felt a creeping shiver run up my spine.

Graur must have felt uneasiness too because he said, "There's nothing good in this place, Annabelle. I can smell the evil here. It's so potent. It slices into my heart and mind and tries to corrupt everything I love."

"I know. I feel it, too. We'll try to hurry and get done what we've come to do. I certainly don't want to stay here any longer than necessary."

I'd decided to leave the canoe halfway beached. I didn't think there was a need to hide the canoe because our visit would only be brief. Besides, I didn't want to drag it from a hiding spot just in case our getaway was going to be lightning-fast with an army on our heels.

I then realized that hiding the canoe would have been pointless anyway. Three canoes were in a small clearing a dozen yards from the water. It made me wonder how many times those canoes transported captured children from our group to this place.

"I think the Jade Army has frequently visited our island. Think about it for a second. Every time one of our friends is taken, Simora has to be the one to strip them of every decent emotion they have. Then she must summon members of the army to come and take away the newest members. So if her power is limited to our island, then we are constantly in close company with members of the army," I said, as we quietly moved down the curving path to somewhere unknown.

"If they can easily land on our island, then why haven't they ever mounted an attack? Why wouldn't they capture and force the rest of you into their army? Why do they even bother leaving a resisting force?" Graur said.

"Maybe they need us for some reason. I guess Simora needs us for some reason since she's the true power behind the Jade Army. Maybe it's like having a large platter of food in front of you. If this platter were the only food source for a long time, you wouldn't eat it all at once. The logical thing to do would be to take a bite only when the need was there. Perhaps that's why the Jade Army doesn't take everyone when they destroy a ship. They take the strongest people first and leave the rest to survive until Simora needs them," I said.

"You may be right, Annabelle," Graur said.

As we followed the path into the thickening forest, I began to dread where this path ended. I was sure we wouldn't find overly friendly people harvesting crops, building necessary shelter, or even weaving fabric for new clothing, as was our focus on the other island. I figured here we might find many people manufacturing weapons and maybe training military tactics. I even thought there would be others huddled in a circle studying a map that would show their next strategic move.

We crept to the base of a large tree and peered down the hill. At the bottom was a lagoon cut into the island. Floating beside a long wooden dock was the three-mast green ship I had seen slip from the fog and destroy our boat three weeks before. What I saw shocked me to the core. The group of people must have totaled nearly three hundred men, women, and children. It had to be the entire Jade Army gathered for a rally of some kind. It honestly looked like they were preparing for a massive attack. My sight then traveled to the treetops and studied something hovering above the group.

"Graur, please tell me that the thing in the trees is just my imagination."

Graur's eyes rotated from the army's group to the thick treetops. His reflexes quickly made him draw back in shock.

"I see it, Annabelle, but I'm not sure of what it is I'm looking at," Graur whispered.

"I think I can confidently say that's the biggest damn spider I've ever seen," I whispered back.

In the treetops were thick strands of silk-like white webbing. Within that enormous web was a spider that could have easily matched its size to an elephant. The thing was midnight black and had dozens of orange spots covering the bulbous section of its body. Its legs twitched

131

every few seconds. The movement caused the web to shake, making the entire forest canopy move.

"You were right in the beginning. This quest was a terrible idea," I told Graur.

I started pulling back from our covered position but stopped when I heard a voice speaking loud and in a commanding tone. I recognized that voice, so did Graur because we quickly caught each other's eyes in a look of puzzlement.

When I crawled forward again, I saw Nate standing on a platform in the center of this large group. His voice was the one we recognized. He was wearing clothing that had a clean look compared to the ragged garments the rest of the crowd wore. He designed his clothes as a type of leader might, ranking himself higher above all the others.

"No, that's impossible. I just left Nate."

"Annabelle, that's Roland, Nate's twin brother," Graur said.

Graur immediately knew that my mind was trying to figure out how Nate had somehow beaten us to this island, how he had an unlikely place within the Jade Army. I'd completely forgotten when Jasmine told me last night about Nate's twin brother under Simora's power. This boy was the person Jasmine suspected of being the Jade King.

I thought of how coincidental it was. Simora and Lothlora are twin sisters who parted ways because good and evil had no chance to coexist. Nate and his twin brother also parted ways in similar circumstances. Nate spent his time on the island to improve the unfortunate situation for the entire group. Roland's focus was primarily on seizing control of all those who resisted. When Roland wandered into Simora's domain, the good that was in him instantly stolen, and now only evil remained.

As I looked closer, I realized that they weren't identical. I noticed subtle differences in Roland's features that I couldn't find in Nate's. Roland also had differences that weren't genetic but markings made by the hand of life. Roland has a thin, jagged scar running through his left eyebrow and down his cheek. His skin was sallow as if his body ridden with an incurable disease. The thing I noticed most of all was the hardness of his eyes. His eye contact with each member of the army was brief and without concern. It was in those eyes that I was sure he felt nothing for the people here.

"The day has finally come. Our soldier, who has willingly lived with the enemy for over a year, has reported back. We know that the enemy has built a ship of their own. They've kept its construction hidden in a cavern on the southern part of the island. This ship is nearly ready. Tomorrow morning our entire army will set sail with a heading for this secret lair. I want all of you to join me on our ship as we witness the destruction of their pride and efforts. Our cannons will blast away the island's entire southern face until the walls crumble down on them. When we discover this ship, we'll obliterate the vessel before it's able to leave this hidden port. No one of the group is permitted to leave the island. We are the rulers of the islands, the sea, and those who travel to our world," Roland shouted.

A roaring cheer rose from the large crowd. It was the worst kind of rally.

"They know about the Good Ship, Graur. They're going to destroy it tomorrow. We have to warn the others as soon as possible," I whispered.

As I slowly and quietly pushed myself off my stomach and to my feet, my eyes landed on faces I hadn't expected to see again. My sight found the faces of my father and brother among the mass of people. They were standing close to Roland and cheered along with the others. Their expressions were ones I didn't recognize ever seeing. It was a look matching the lifelessness of all the others.

"Graur, it's my father and brother. They're alive!"

"Whatever ideas are going through your mind right now must be forgotten, Annabelle. You were right to say that your friends need to be informed about the upcoming attack. Even the children taken last night are out of our control. We must take the canoe and return to the other island. If we risk trying to save someone who doesn't want to be saved, then we chance being captured. If we get captured, your friends will never know of the upcoming attack. They could face possible death by the morning light if we're unable to return with this news," Graur said.

I reluctantly pulled my eyes from my father and brother and looked at Graur. His illuminating green eyes were soft and caring. He could see my inner struggle. I wanted to throw away everything to save my family from the evil hand of the Jade Army. However, I knew that without a doubt, the army would capture us. I would become part of their group. Graur would be put to death. After all the years of placing hope and faith into building the ship, I didn't have the right to step aside and let something so beautiful die.

"You're right. We must get back to the island. We must let the others know about what's coming tomorrow morning," I said.

When Graur and I turned to go, we were facing the business end of two swords.

"Well, look what we found. I would have thought that your numbers for an offensive attack would be much, much larger," said one of the filthy boys.

<u>18</u>

Run for Your Life

Graur was lightning fast as he dodged to the left in a roll, sprang to his feet, and clamped his jaws tightly on the wrist of one of the boys brandishing a sword. The blonde-haired boy threw his head back and released a howl of pain echoing throughout the woods.

The boy holding the sword an inch in front of my nose turned in surprise. As he drew his arm back, prepared to bring the blade down on Graur's exposed neck, I reared my arm back and swung my fist with the most velocity I could have ever conjured. The blow connected with the boy's left temple and pin-wheeled him unconsciously to the dirt path.

Graur struggled to keep a hold on the other boy's arm when I stepped behind the kid and drove my elbow into the back of his head. He crumpled to his knees and then slumped forward into the foliage.

I massaged my arm. The strike had sent a bolt of spikes across my nerves. I stooped and collected one of the dropped swords. I checked its weight by swinging it from side to side.

"Are you all right, Annabelle?" Graur asked.

"Yeah, we need to go."

I glanced down the path and saw three hundred faces looking back at me. The scream from the blonde boy had alerted the entire Jade Army.

The worst thing of all was that the creature high in the trees resembling a massive spider began bouncing on the webs. The forest ceiling covering the Jade Army began shaking as the spider's bouncing weight tested the strength of all the trees connected to the gigantic web. I wasn't sure if this action from the spider was out of anger or excitement. I honestly didn't care to find out.

Graur and I turned and ran.

It wasn't a sound that could be easily blocked out, not even by the pounding of my feet on the dirt path. What we heard was a tidal wave of flesh, bone, and roaring hate. The swell of bodies raced up the hill to where we had been moments before.

"Nanum ra saylore bae lo hasslun." It was a whispering voice, seeming to come from absolutely everywhere.

"What was that? Was that the spider-thing talking?" I asked as my speed quicken.

"Whatever it was, it sounded like whispers of death," Graur said.

Graur certainly had a way with words. I thought that his statement somehow cursed us because the earth in front of us came alive a moment later. I only took a glance as we sped past. I could have sworn that the ground was transforming into some hideous shape. It was like the ground was liquefying and bubbling up from the pressure below. A dozen mounds contorted and formed as we weaved a path between them.

I looked over my shoulder. The erupting mounds spit out the sinister creations. Graur and I now had a dozen grotesquely hairy spiders the size of deer quickly shuffling along the path behind us.

Oh, my God, I thought.

The awful creatures were fast. They were gaining ground with eagerness. Even at the sight of them, I still felt my energy depleting. I didn't think we had a chance to make it to the canoe. I now realized how incompetent my mission was all along.

When I risked another glance over my shoulder, I saw one directly behind me. Its beady black eyes focused on me. The pincers at its mouth worked rapidly. It was probably relishing with anticipation of the taste of my insides.

I leaped to the left as the spider lunged for me. I drew back the sword and chopped at its front legs. In a sweeping arch, the blade cut directly through three of its legs. The spider crumpled, and to my amazement, the thing tumbled and blew apart in a brown cloud. As I looked again, I realized that the spiders hadn't been lying in wait beneath the dirt, suddenly summoned by their master's call. They were born of dirt, leaves, and fallen branches.

The collapse of the spider acted like an accident on a busy highway. One of the spiders collided with the broken clumps of dirt. That fragmenting spider then took out two more. Behind us was a large cloud, which looked like a raging sandstorm heading right for us.

"Dirt! The spiders are only dirt, Graur!" I said excitedly.

"Faster, Annabelle."

Ahead I could see the end of the path and the water beyond. I heard something quickly moving behind us. I looked back. I saw one of the spiders had avoided the pile-up by cutting a path through the trees. As it sped up to us, I abruptly turned and brought the sword down on the center of its bulbous body. The dirt exploded around me. In the dust cloud, I could hear a terror coming alive in the forest.

Graur was eagerly waiting for me at the canoe. He was anxiously bounding from side to side like a child throwing a quiet tantrum.

As I approached, I hooked my hand on the canoe's end and quickly pulled it into the water. I leaped in, and Graur followed. I substituted my sword for an oar and began frantically paddling for the other island.

"If you have the talent to somehow paddle, now is the time to show it," I said as I stroked the water.

"They also have canoes. When we get to the island, I'll follow you to the well so that you can find the safety of the cavern, and then I'll retreat to my home," Graur said.

We glanced back to study the shore. Several spiders reached the end of the path and bounced in frustration at our escape. One of them ignorantly tested the water with its front legs, the dirt sucked up the salty water, and its legs broke off in muddy clumps. With its balance thrown off, the spider pitched forward into the water. A wide, brown cloud appeared on the surface.

The Jade Army appeared at the shore. They pulled the three beached canoes into the water, and four kids loaded in each. They were strong and determined, as the speed of their canoes was faster than ours. In a matter of minutes, they would catch us.

I began to feel hope fading. I was ready to give up until something orange and white and enormous broke from the water. Its long rubbery tentacles shot straight into the air. With only the force a creature from the deep blue sea could manage, it brought its power down onto two canoes' front ends. Eight boys were catapulted into the air and then crashed into the water. The flailing tentacles skipped across the water and pulverized the remaining canoe. The twelve boys that were consumed with hate only moments ago suddenly found a different emotion. Fear had overtaken them as they realized that something more powerful and far more ruthless was in the water with them. They scrambled through the water like rats fleeing a sinking ship.

I continued to paddle as we watched the attack with astonishment. I was also waiting with the nervous expectation of our canoe violently getting hurled in the air. For whatever reason behind its plan, the sea creature allowed us safe passage back to our island.

I didn't think that it was the entire Jade Army in pursuit of us. Maybe only a quarter of them. On the beach was an angry crowd of people, a few fidgety dirt spiders, and twelve exhausted boys pulling themselves onto the land. The three canoes bobbed on the water in shattered pieces. There was no chance of them crossing anytime soon. For now, we were safe.

I pulled the canoe onto the shore, and Graur jumped out. I grabbed my backpack and said, "Let's go."

We didn't run because we didn't have the energy. Instead, Graur and I made a slow and steady pace back to base camp. I had the desire to stop and rest, but I knew that the information we had on the Jade Army's current plan of action tomorrow morning had to be revealed to the rest of the group as soon as possible.

"What was that big spider? It somehow spoke those words like a spell and brought the ground to life to capture us. Those spiders were only dirt, sticks, and leaves, nothing more," I said.

"It's almost like Simora, only different in some ways."

"Yeah, that's what I was thinking. Instead of a giant serpent, it was a giant spider, capable of being in the daylight, and just as creepy," I said.

"It's apparent that the Jade Army has many powerful allies. We were fortunate enough to escape their island," Graur said.

"Whatever that spider creature is, I'm glad it's an island away. If that thing were here, our group would never stand a chance against it and Simora."

Sunlight passed into the everlasting blue waters when we reached base camp, or what remained of our base camp. Something completely destroyed everything I've come to love about the campgrounds.

We walked beneath the towering trees, mystified by the shambles of camp. There were cut ropes, broken slats of wood, and destroyed possessions everyone had collected over time. Somehow, someone or something smashed nearly every hut high in the branches. The rubble had fallen in a heap to the ground. Our crops were now a mangled mess. Everything about this place that made it home for us was now in ruins.

"What unearthly creation could do this kind of destruction?" Graur asked.

Neither of us knew the answer to that question.

"Hello?" I called out.

No one responded to my shouts.

"There's nothing left. How can we possibly rebuild all this?" I asked but then realized I already knew the answer. We weren't going to rebuild. We were going to board the Good Ship and flee this place.

I thought of my failure at attempting to get my friends back from the other island.

141

"I can't do anything right, Graur. I've disappointed everyone who has ever put their faith and trust in me," I said and lowered my head.

Graur approached me and said, "Annabelle, in the short time we've known each other, I have to say that you're the bravest and most determined young person I've ever met."

"How can you say that when I failed everything I set out to do?"

"Honestly, I was sure the journey would be for nothing. I believe in your heart that you knew that as well. I know that once Simora strips the good from someone, there's no getting it back. At least not while you're all here in this place and time. Once you pass through the gateway, maybe everything she has stolen from each person is returned. I can't say for sure. I can only hope. The failure of our mission is a matter of perspective. Perhaps we didn't recover those taken last night, but we learned a great deal from the enemy," Graur said.

"You mean about the attack tomorrow?"

"Yes. If you hadn't gone on your quest, then you and your friends would suffer the terrible wrath of the Jade Army in the morning. Right now, you have a chance to place the odds in your favor. You must hurry and tell others this news. The light is fading, and time grows short. It's now time for us to say goodbye, Annabelle."

Graur was right. I had information that could determine our fate. I had knowledge that could save the lives of my friends.

I crouched and wrapped my arms around Graur's neck. He nuzzled my cheek.

"I wish you could come with us," I said.

"This is my home, Annabelle. I believe when your plans are complete, our world will be rid of Simora once and for all. This place will be good again."

"I'm going to miss you, Graur," I said as we parted.

"And I will miss you just as much, Annabelle. Tell the others that I wish all of you a safe journey home. You must get to the ship as quickly as possible. Go now, and don't look back."

I stroked his head as tears began building in my eyes. I turned and ran for the well. I didn't look back.

19

The Worst Things to Come

There's a certain eeriness about the forest in the growing dark, especially when alone. I stormed through clouds of bugs hovering in the path as I hastily ran for the well. It was difficult keeping my mind from the destruction of the camp. I couldn't imagine what had caused the mayhem in broad daylight. The members of base camp always had a small arsenal in preparation for an attack. Whatever damaged the huts high in the trees must have been injured or possibly destroyed. The lack of witnesses or evidence of the outcome bothered me. No one was left behind to tell the story.

At the opposite end of the open field, I saw the silhouette of the well. No one was standing guard. No one waited for me. It was now evident that the entire topside of the island was void of all my friends. The attack must have forced any survivors to retreat to the dark and practically barren cavern. It was the only place left to make a last stand if we could not set the Good Ship to sail by early tomorrow morning.

I approached the well. Someone lowered the bucket. Whoever was the last person to seek the cavern's safety must have slid down the rope like a fireman's pole.

When I climbed the wall of the well and sat on the edge, I felt something crawling at the base of my neck. My hand was already in motion when Nate's words came calling back to me from weeks before. It was a simple warning completely forgotten.

I felt a spike of pain shoot across my nerves as my hand smashed the thing creeping on my skin. It wasn't pain caused by my hand smacking the sensitive area but had instead been the bite of an insect. My fingers gripped the flattened insect. I held it in front of me so I could verify what I already suspected. The insect landing on me was what the children called a black and blue beetle. I carefully studied the squashed insect to make sure. It was a dime-sized black beetle with a pale blue death's head on its back. It was the insect that caused the unfortunate seven-year flu. A single bite from the beetle can bring someone seven years of persistent illness.

It seems to be my strange way through life that I would stumble into a train wreck of bad luck like this on the eve of our escape.

I heard a thundering roll of something running through the forest. I wasn't sure how long I had stared at that squashed beetle, but now the warning sounds of approaching hunters brought me back to reality. Darkness had settled in quickly. I wiped the beetle's remains on the stones of the well. I used my shirtsleeves to grip the rope. I also entangled my feet around the rope as a way to control my descent. I threw my weight from the wall and rapidly slid down into the still darkness.

I hit the bottom of the well with a jarring speed forceful enough to splinter apart the bucket on the cavern floor. My body crumpled into a tangled heap.

Something howled from somewhere like a million miles away. When I looked up into the hovering blackness, I fully expected to see half a dozen black shadows with glowing blue eyes and gleaming white teeth falling down the well on top of me. After a moment, I realized that following me must have been impossible for them.

I'm now in the only place on the entire island we could consider safe. At least it would be safe until tomorrow morning.

A wave of dizziness overcame me as I stood. At the back of my neck was a fire beneath the skin. It felt like a warm tingle at first and then quickly heated as if my blood were flammable and had ignited.

My balance wobbled as I made my way down the winding pathway to the cavern floor. The dizziness hadn't lifted but had intensified. I spotted groups of kids at the small clusters of campsites. I could see the fires burning brightly and the children surrounding them. As I stumbled down the path, I noticed that several of the groups saw me coming. They stood, hazy silhouettes in the distance that watched me with curiosity. Dozens of them moved toward me with torches in hand.

"Annabelle?" a girl with a sweet, concerned voice said.

"I don't feel so good after all," I said to the crowd. The blurriness in my eyes prevented me from focusing on a single face.

"Hey, move aside, you guys." It was a voice I recognized.

"Nate, is that you?"

"Oh, my God. Annabelle?" I saw a figure shove through the lingering bodies.

I felt incredibly weak, and my knees gave out. I went down softly because a dozen hands suddenly reached out to catch me. A cool hand brushed the damp hair from my forehead. Nate's face moved in close. I could see that he was smiling.

"I can't believe it. Where have you been?" Nate asked.

"I did something foolish. Graur and I went to the northern island to try and get back those eight children. I wanted to get them back because I messed up so badly. We found a canoe and paddled across the ocean. You wouldn't even believe what we saw. Is it hot in here?" I asked as my entire body felt overheated, as if I'd just spent the day sunbathing.

"No, it's quite cool down here. You don't look so good, Annabelle."

"I remembered your warning. I remembered what you told me when I first came here. You told me not to slap at those things. You said they would only bite if they felt threatened. It was only a habit to slap at something crawling on me, but it had got me before I squashed it."

"What bit you, Annabelle?" another voice asked me.

My mind was having a hard time working at average speeds. I couldn't seem to access parts of my memory as fast as usual.

"One of those beetles landed on my neck. What are they called? Oh, yeah, a black and blue beetle. It bit me and set my skin on fire."

"Annabelle, when did it bite you? How long ago?" Nate asked.

"Oh, a few minutes ago. Before I came down the well, the beetle latched on like an angry thing. I suppose if someone had slapped at me, I probably would have done the same thing."

"The venom acts quickly. A few minutes might be enough time to get some of it out. I have to do something, Annabelle. It's going to hurt, but I have to do something before it's too late. There's nothing I can do about the venom already running through your veins. I still have a chance to work some of it out of the bite area. Here, hold on tightly to my left hand," Nate said.

I took his hand. With his other hand, he gently turned my head to expose the bite mark. He withdrew the knife from his belt and leaned in closer. I fully expected him to kiss me again, his mouth pulling in so close. Instead, I felt a thundering jab of pain coursing throughout my body. My muscles convulsed as if every nerve ending in my body was stuck with a needle. I released a scream that pushed back all of the hovering faces and echoed my pain across the cavern.

I tried to take my mind from the situation. My eyes found a small gap in the group of children. I could see the beautifully constructed ship beyond them. It was like a perfectly assembled work of art that no other group of craftsmen around the world could duplicate. I tried to remember that I had something important to tell everyone, but the pain made it hard to figure out precisely what that was.

"They tasted like buttered popcorn," I said.

Nate was still leaning over me. His sight fixed on his current task.

"What did?" he asked.

"The flowers. They tasted just like movie theater buttered popcorn."

"Yeah, I know what you mean. I've eaten the flowers before, too. You hold still and try not to talk."

There was another eruption of pain that caused me to hiss.

"No, I'm having a hard time focusing. That's not what I wanted to tell all of you. When I was on the other island, I overheard him speaking. I thought it was you at first, but

Graur told me that he's your twin brother. I overheard their plans."

Nate stopped what he was doing. He leaned back on his heels and carefully studied me. He brushed my hair from my face again and said, "You mean you saw Roland?"

"Yeah, Roland." I seized Nate's hand with a tight grip and said, "You need to listen to me. All of you need to listen. The Jade Army is planning to attack in the morning. They know everything we've been doing here. They know about the Good Ship and our plans to escape the island. They know the ship is in a hidden cavern somewhere on the southern part of the island, but they don't know the exact location. They'll bombard the entire southern face of the island. The wall won't be able to take much. After a few hits, they'll be able to see exactly where our ship is hiding. Do you hear me? We have to leave by the morning, or their ship will blow ours apart before we can sail it from the cavern."

All of the children were staring at me in disbelief. After a moment, they began turning to each other and rapidly talking.

"Quiet, everyone," I heard Anica shout. "We need to remain calm. It's not the time or place to completely lose our heads."

Nate said, "She's right. We have to focus on what we need to do in the hours before sunrise. It certainly isn't the time we expected to leave. Even though we didn't finish everything we hoped to complete, we don't have a choice in the matter. We have to get everything together as quickly as possible. Before long, we'll have to blow the wall down and force the ship from the cavern. Collect everything you can. Move, you guys, move!"

The group of children parted in different directions. Nate remained behind. He moved my head onto his lap and looked down at me with soft eyes.

"I thought that we lost you. I didn't know what to think when you vanished in the morning. I didn't know if you ran away or if someone took you."

"I guess you could say that I ran away with intentions of coming back with a bunch of people. It was a stupid idea that nearly got Graur and myself killed or captured."

I told Nate everything about our canoe trip to the northern island and the Jade Army's gathering. I told him about the giant spider in the trees, the dirt spiders' pursuit, and our dreadfully close escape assisted by a large orange sea creature.

"So, you're telling me that your day was far more interesting than mine?" Nate asked.

I shrugged.

"I had to cut the area where the beetle bit you. I squeezed out as much of the venom that hadn't yet absorbed into your bloodstream. You're still going to feel some effects of the venom, but nothing near as bad as Max suffered."

Nate helped me to my feet. We began a slow walk to the ship.

"All right, so tell me all about your day," I said.

"Well, did you see what happened to base camp?" Nate asked.

"Yeah, at first, Graur and I figured the Jade Army had attacked sometime during the day, but that wouldn't be possible since they were all on the other island," I said.

"No, the army had nothing to do with that. We were the ones who did the destruction."

I stopped and looked at Nate. "What? Why on earth would you guys do that?"

"It's simple. In the morning, none of us knew for sure about what happened to you. Some of us thought you ran away. Others, like myself, thought the Jade Army kidnapped you during the night. No one was sure if Simora had turned you into one of the members of the army during your capture in her dark nest. We decided that since we planned to leave the island in a little over a week, it's safer for everyone to stay below in the cavern. We took all of the supplies we would need until we left the island. We destroyed most of the stuff topside to create confusion."

"Confusion?" I asked.

"Yeah. Since we didn't know what to expect after you had gone, we decided that we'd throw in an element of misdirection. We thought that after we escaped Simora's nest, maybe the Jade Army would come to our camp. We figured they would show up and be completely dumbfounded by what they found. There would be no way for them to find out what happened to our camp or where we had gone. At the time, we didn't know they've been aware of the cavern and the ship."

"Okay, I get it now. It still must have been hard to tear all of that apart since you guys spent so long constructing everything."

Nate shrugged. "Not really. They were only buildings. We knew everything would remain here anyway."

"So you know, I'm not under Simora's power. She wasn't able to infect me like she did the others," I said.

"I never thought that you were under her control."

"But there's someone in our group who's a traitor. Someone has been informing the army of our progress on the Good Ship and its general whereabouts," I said.

"That doesn't matter anymore. Tomorrow morning we're going to leave this place for good. Right now, we need to help complete everything. So let's get to it," Nate said.

<u>20</u>

Final Preparations

Nate and I were looking through a journal. He would study a page, rapidly flip several pages back, and then return to the original page. He stopped every so often to talk to himself and form an answer and then jotted something down.

I kept from speaking to him so that I wouldn't break his concentration. Nate was calculating the position in which our ship would meet with the gateway to take us home.

Nate had told me some time ago that the gateway works on a mystical, universally constructed clock. It disappears and appears on a constant cycle in different positions around the island. Sometimes it's a great distance from land. Sometimes it's nowhere to be found, but it was reliable regardless of the constant jumping.

"We spent years tracking the gateway and recording its positions. It didn't take long before we figured out that it appears in the same position each day of every calendar year. I can't explain why it does what it does or how it moves as it does, but I can figure out where it will be tomorrow morning. Hopefully, tomorrow isn't one of the rare days we could never find it because its distance from the island was too far. There are only five days out of the year when we can't find it. It could be appearing on the opposite side of the northern island during those times. That might be the reason we couldn't find it during those five days. Ah, here it is. According to the journal, the gateway should be nearly four nautical miles from the northeastern part of the island tomorrow. That means we'll need to sail around the entire island first and then head an additional four nautical miles," Nate said.

"Do you think we can make that?" I asked.

Nate shrugged and said, "It's hard to tell. The Jade Army will probably be blasting away at us with their firepower as we make a run for it. We planned on waiting a bit longer before leaving because the gateway will be the closest to the southern part of the island. It would be the prime moment for a clean getaway. I guess that desperate times call for desperate measures. We no longer have a choice of when we depart from the island."

I was staring at the deck of the ship, lost in thought as I tried to figure out a nearly impossible decision requiring an immediate answer.

"Is something wrong?" Nate asked, reading the worry on my face.

"You weren't truthful to me about seeing my family again, were you? Every time I asked you about the plan of getting them back, you always changed the subject or said that you had something to do."

Nate hung his head and said, "I lied to you, Annabelle. You were so crushed when I found you on the beach. I just wanted to lift your spirits. I wanted to give you some hope to keep you going. I'm sorry. I was wrong to lie. We never really had a plan of getting anyone back. Something like that seems nearly impossible when we're facing an army of three hundred or more."

"It's all right. I think I knew all along that there wasn't a plan. I don't hold it against you for trying to give me hope. I think you're great for what you said, but I've been thinking a lot about all of the others. I've been thinking about my father, brother, and all of the others forced into the Jade Army. None of those people are bad because they want to be. They've all become victims under Simora's power."

"I know that, Annabelle. I can't get my family out of my head. I feel like I'm abandoning them to save myself. From where we stand, I can't see a possible solution for defeating an entire army and a force like Simora," Nate said.

"I think I have an idea. I might have thought of a way where all of us can escape together. It's not a solid plan yet. It needs some serious figuring out. There's a chance that all of us can leave this place."

Nate was looking at me with extreme interest.

"I'm listening," he said.

I laid out the rough draft of my idea in conversation and grammar school sketches I scribbled in the journal. Nate nodded and occasionally offered other methods of seeing the concept to the final stages. There wasn't anything spectacular about the plan, but if it fell in step at the right time, then it would be significant enough to do as Nate and I hoped it would.

"Okay, I'm going to get this drawing to Jacob. I'll have him forge these as quickly as possible. There should be plenty of time before we have to leave. I want you to help the others gather the rest of the stuff we need and get everything secured in the ship. Make sure everyone is buckling down all of the loose objects. We don't know the conditions of the ocean today. It might be a rough ride. Plus, there's the possibility of cannon fire from the Jade

Army that could send things not strapped down flying around. I don't want anyone injured if we can avoid it."

"I'll take care of it. I'll see you soon," I said and kissed Nate's cheek.

I spent the better part of the next two hours doing as Nate had asked of me. I helped those coming up the flight of stairs to find a home for their personal belongings. A bit later, I was satisfied after a thorough check of each room. I left the ship and headed for the wall separating us from the ocean.

I circled the hull, inspecting the integrity of the structure when I ran into Cody. The boy nominated as the explosives expert years before now studied a cluster of wires.

I smiled and said, "Hey, Cody, are you making last-minute inspections also?"

"Yeah, Annabelle. I must have checked everything a thousand times. All it takes is a single oversight to ruin the plan. I certainly don't want to be the one responsible for keeping us trapped in here as the Jade Army blasts away at our ship."

"I completely understand. I've fouled up several times during my short stay here. I made a stupid mistake, and because of it, eight of our friends are gone from our group. I keep wondering how I can ever make things right," I said.

"To be honest, I think there's more pressure on me right now than ever before. I've got to bring down the entire wall and then blow out the back wall and bring the river in with precise timing and accuracy. If we've somehow miscalculated these walls' thickness, then the explosives I've packed in them won't be enough. We'll be nothing more than sitting ducks."

I looked into Cody's eyes and said, "We all have confidence in you. I don't doubt that you made sure everything is accurate. I'll leave you to it."

I decided to find Nate and Jacob. I wanted to see how the new plan was coming along. I was pretty sure that they must be finishing up on the project. I was eager to see the results.

Only a few hours passed since I came down the well and spoke of the dire situation we'd be facing tomorrow. Now the cavern seemed void of all the people who had come to me along the path. There were only a few unimportant things we left behind at each of the camps.

I saw a bright red glow near the cavern's back and knew that Nate and Jacob were still working on completing the project. The forging area was scorching, immediately forcing sweat from my skin. It was like walking into a pit of molten lava.

"How are things coming?" I asked as I approached.

Nate looked up and said, "Great. We're quenching the last one now."

I studied one of the giant three-pronged metal hooks.

"Just as I earlier thought, they are simple but yet effective if used properly. Did you tell Jacob the reason for making these?"

Jacob said, "Yeah, he did. Huge fish hooks, only for catching a ship instead of a monster fish. I love the idea. I'm glad both of you created this plan of action to get our families back. Like you, and probably everyone else down here, I don't think I could live with the idea of leaving my family behind when we can do something to get them back."

"I honestly think it'll work," Nate offered.

I sat down on a boulder and wiped the sweat from my face. I was feeling awful during the last few hours since the black and blue bit me. I had a cold sweat, blurred vision, and a hard time finding focus.

"Are you okay, Annabelle?" Nate asked.

"The venom is starting to kick into a higher gear. I'm not feeling so well right now. I'm exhausted."

Nate said, "Can you finish up things by yourself, Jacob?"

"Yeah. I just need to secure cables to these. I'll bring everything to the ship in a little while."

"Great. I'm going to get Annabelle back to the ship to rest for a bit before we have to leave," Nate said.

I wrapped my arm around his shoulders. We made slow progress down the path to the ship.

I started to laugh a little as we walked along the cavern floor.

Nate smiled at my sudden mood change. He said, "What is it? What's so funny?"

"Oh, I just had a major flash go through my mind about all the things I've dealt with in the short time since I landed here."

"It's just like any ordinary island, I'm sure. Pirates, moving trees, black shadows with teeth kidnapping children, dirt spiders, sorry I missed those, by the way, and a creature more powerful than all of the others combined," Nate teased.

"You forgot about the talking wolf-like creature named Graur, those little fairies you call mischief, an assortment of strange sea creatures, and buttered popcorn flavored flowers. There's probably more, but I can't think of them right now," I said.

"I'd say you've had yourself a busy and extraordinarily unusual few weeks. Hopefully, tomorrow we won't finish out your time here with a bang and another plunge into the ocean."

We made our way to the ship's deck and down the stairs to one of the empty rooms. Nate left me for a moment. I slid onto the bed and closed my eyes. A minute later, I felt a cool, damp cloth pressed to my forehead. I opened my eyes to see Nate caring for me as if I were his sick grandmother.

"Despite everything that's happened, I'm glad you came here to the island," Nate whispered.

"I'm glad, too. I've never had a friend like you before," I said and drifted off to unsettling dreams.

21

The Wall Comes Down

Distant thunder woke me a short while later. I lay in the comfortable bed and stared into the darkness. My body was still achy, but the fever and nausea seemed to diminish during my rest. I sat up and listened to the thunder drawing closer. I was amazed that I could hear the rumble, considering I was deep inside the ship and quite a distance in the cavern.

I heard commotion overhead when I pushed myself from the bed and found a steady balance. Heavy footfalls were stamping down on the deck of the ship. It sounded like a marching squad had boarded, and they were in the middle of a performance.

Kids almost trampled me as I made my way up the stairs to the deck. A small troop of kids went crashing down the stairs past me and into the belly of the ship.

"What's going on? What's your hurry?" I called after them.

No one answered. The four children parted in different directions when they hit the bottom of the steps. I climbed faster, as I felt the need to discover the reason for the chaos as quickly as possible. I was looking for chaos, and chaos is what I found.

The entire deck of the ship was alive as a mass of bodies shuffled around. There were groups of kids unfolding and securing the sails to each mast. Other groups were busy finishing the final load of all possessions. I could see several people in the darkness of the cavern floor at the bow of the ship. I thought that Nate was one of them.

I leaned over the rail and said, "Nate, is that you?"

"Annabelle, you need to get below. Go back to the bedroom and stay there until I come for you," Nate called to me.

"What's going on? Why is everyone in a panic?"

"The Jade Army is attacking. They're blasting away at the southern cliffs. It's time to leave this place."

That was when I realized that it wasn't thundering at all, but the sounds of cannon fire.

"I want to help. What can I do?" I urgently called down to Nate.

I saw Nate's shoulders sag as he realized that I wasn't going to run and hide in a room while everyone else prepared to set the ship to sail.

"All right, come down here and help us finish wiring the explosives."

I almost paused to ask if there was perhaps something else I could do. With my streak of rotten luck lately, I was sure to prematurely set off the explosions and kill us all before the Jade Army had their chance. I figured I could at least supervise the dangerous task.

I bounded down the stairs and found Nate and Jacob huddled under a torch that lit the area at the base of the wall. They had groups of wires running from different wall sections to another cluster of wires at our feet. Jacob took wires from Nate and started twisting them together.

After the connection of wires, Jacob handed me the spool and said, "I want you to run this up the stairs. Take it to the control panel next to the captain's wheel, where Cody is working. You'll need to feed out the wire as you go. Be careful not to snag on anything. One loose wire could undo the entire setup, and then we would be in serious trouble."

Nate and I fixed our sight on each other for a long moment. I figure we were both thinking that I wasn't the proper person for such a tremendous chore. I was going to screw it up somehow, someway, no doubt.

"You can do this, Annabelle," Nate said, much to my surprise. He leaned in and kissed me gently.

"Great, we're about to be blown to smithereens, and you two are making out. Perfect timing if ever there was one," Jacob said with a smirk.

"We have to finalize the explosives at the back of the cavern. Wait for us on deck. It shouldn't take us more than a few minutes," Nate said.

I carefully unraveled the spool as I walked back to the stairs. I stumbled a few times on small boulders but regained my balance before falling. Maneuvering the staircase was a trick in itself. I had to manage the length of wire dangling over the edge while trying to work my way up each flight of steps. I thought that if I tugged too hard, the explosive charges would be ripped from the wall and make our escape attempt a worthless endeavor.

Sometimes the belief in my abilities to accomplish simple tasks hangs on a long, single thread. It usually doesn't take much to strain the thread enough to its breaking point. Nate and Jacob showed me immense confidence in this responsibility. This small gesture helped rebuild the self-worth that I had lost somewhere along the way.

162

I would have made them proud. The spool of wires reached the deck of the ship without becoming snagged or cut during transport. I found Cody working on the control panel housing the electronics that would ignite the charges. I crouched next to him. Cody removed the top section of the panel and adjusted some of the inner workings.

"Jacob and Nate wanted me to set the wires up here and wait for them to come back," I said as I placed the coil beside the panel.

"Great. You can leave it there, and I'll get to it in a second. Where are Jacob and Nate now?" he asked.

"At the back of the cavern, running the wires for the charges to blow out the river wall. They said they would only be a few minutes."

"I hope so. Those cannons sound like they're getting mighty close. Can you grab that torch and give me a little more light? I don't want to wire any of these incorrectly and risk screwing up the order of the detonation."

I removed the torch from its wedged position and moved it closer.

"You do know what you're doing, don't you? I think it would be bad to prematurely detonate the explosives when we're not all on board yet," I said.

"Oh, yeah. Jacob and I designed the systems of this box. We've used it many times over the years. We've taken that wall down to practically nothing. It used to be around ten feet thick, but now it's probably only a couple of feet. The wall is so thin now that I'm amazed it's still standing after all these years. I think Jacob and I currently have enough explosives in that wall to blow it three times over. When I flick these switches, there will be a small current of electricity traveling through the wires. Inside each of our charges is a small flare-like device that activates when the electrical current reaches it. When that little flare lights up, it turns into a small ball of fire and ignites the chemicals within each charge, and then boom, baby," Cody said.

"Hey, we have the rest of them here," Jacob said, coming up behind us.

Jacob slid in beside Cody. They worked quickly but methodically as they attached the wires in the designated order to be triggered. It took them less than a minute to complete the task.

"We're good to go, Nate," Cody said.

Anica stepped up behind our small group and said, "I hope you all have some good news for me because the sands of time are almost out."

"The explosives are ready. Have the final preparations been made?" Nate asked her.

"Everyone's ready when you guys are," she said.

"I guess that's it then. It's time to finally bring the wall down and let the river shoot us from the cavern. It's time to break free from this world or die trying," Jacob said as he closed the top panel on the box.

We all stared at that panel with the dozens of toggle switches that would ignite the explosives. Then I thought that each of us was silently praying to God or praying to the universal creation of good luck. I figured we could use all the help we could get.

"Okay. Nate, let's get all those who don't need to be up here below deck," Anica said.

They split off to gather the rest of the children, running them to the lower levels to safer territory. Anica and Nate came back a minute later and gave Cody a nod to confirm that we were as ready as we'll ever be.

Cody quickly placed wads of cotton in his ears. He said, "I'd find a good place to brace yourself and cover

164

your heads until the river breaks us out of here. Everyone should stay low. I can't be sure how much rock debris will blow toward us. You better hunker behind something strong and cover your ears because the explosions are going to echo like crazy."

All of us did as instructed. Nate and I crouched behind the mainmast. My heart was hammering so painfully that I could feel my pulse at the bottom of my feet. I had a terrifying vision that we would be blown to tiny pieces when Cody started flipping switches.

We silently watched Cody. He took a moment to double-check that all of us had taken cover. He placed each thumb on the first and second toggle switches and flicked them.

I heard the switches click, and then an explosion rocked the cavern. I felt the shockwave hit like a freight train and forced the air from my lungs.

Cody hurriedly continued with the sequence as he flipped the switches two at a time. He waited no more than two seconds before moving to the next set of switches.

Even with my hands clamped over my ears, it seemed like my eardrums would rupture. I thought maybe even my head would blow apart from the pressure. It seemed like a lifetime passed by when the last explosion finally faded. I saw Cody pull his hands away from the panel. He peered over the edge of the deck to see the results of his masterpiece. What I saw on his features was only something I could describe as delight.

Even without seeing his face, I would have known the results. The cavern was no longer midnight black but flooded with the morning sun's rays reflecting off the water. I even smelled the delightful salty ocean air.

All of us slowly stood and took in the visual finale to Cody's moment of chaos.

There was a massive jagged hole in the wall. Beyond the thick dust was majestic scenery. The sea was calm. The sky was a cloudless tranquil blue. If it hadn't been for the green-colored ship that I knew was just out of sight, I would have sworn that it would be a perfect day for sailing.

Cody finished his quick inspection of the doorway in the cavern wall and ran back to the panel.

"It's a good blast! Exactly as we set it up. The ship should clear the hole on all sides. Everyone get back down and grab hold of something and prepare to get wet!" Cody shouted excitedly.

He began to flick the second row of switches rapidly. I didn't see the smile leave his face even when the explosions started.

The next series of explosions rumbled from the back of the cavern. These were less severe than the first but still jarring enough for me to hope it would be over quickly.

I don't know why I did it, but for an insane moment, I stood from my crouched position. I looked into the depths of the cavern and saw a river running wild toward us. Morning sunlight reflected off the rushing water. The rolling, breaking waves looked like a thousand galloping white horses racing for freedom.

"Are you crazy, Annabelle?" Nate yelled at me while gripping my shirt and pulling me back down.

"Yeah, but so is this entire situation," I yelled back, and laughter escaped me.

I held onto the mast lines as a tidal wave smashed into the stern of the ship. Massive streams of water surged up the ship's hull onto the deck and immediately soaked us.

We all rocked backward as the ship brutally shoved forward.

The Good Ship was making her maiden voyage.

We closely watched the seemingly narrow gap between the port and starboard sides and the jagged rock wall. I studied the small space between the top of the three masts and the angled cut at the top of the hole. A quick mental calculation told me that we'd make it through with little problems.

Or so I thought.

22

An Imperfect Plan

It's a matter of understanding that when operations as complex as this unfold, it becomes commonplace for the unfortunate circumstances in life to step right in.

As our hopes rose, the unseen cruel little demons riding the waves of cause and effect came into play. The enormous amount of water pressure from behind began hammering relentlessly more on the starboard side of the ship. This action then began turning us. The bow was creeping dangerously close to the right side of the rock wall.

Nate sprang up, stumbled, regained balance, and staggered for the captain's wheel. The spinning wheel rapidly beat his hands as he tried to get a grip. When the rudder was momentarily motionless, causing the wheel to cease its spin, Nate clutched the large wooden wheel. He fought the forces of the water, which were far greater than him. He was quickly losing the fight.

I stood from my position behind the mast and went to Nate's side. My hands clamped on the wheel. I used what strength I had to help him regain control of the ship. Anica joined us, and a moment later, we were in a straight line again.

The only problem was that the ship had already shifted too much to one side of the opening.

We were going to hit the wall.

"Brace yourselves!" Anica shouted.

The ship practically came to a complete halt when the port side struck the rock wall. The broken edges of the wall bit into the wood and wouldn't let us go. The tremendous pressure of the rushing river behind us was now pushing the stern to an awkward angle. In moments, we would be permanently stuck in the opening of the cavern.

So far, it had been a perfect plan to get us killed. The Jade Army couldn't have prayed for a better chance to blow us from the water.

As the three of us fought the wheel, I thought of everything I've learned since my arrival. I thought of the hard times each of the children has faced since becoming shipwrecked. The children were once thrown into situations far beyond the limits of their knowledge. Each of them has faced and conquered all challenges day after day on the island. They had built shelters high in the trees, grew extensive gardens, and constructed this incredible ship to sail us home. They've faced the worst adversity any person should ever battle in one hundred lifetimes.

It wasn't time to die. It wasn't time to give up everything we've sacrificed. It wasn't time to see this beautiful ship destroyed by those whose minds are warped by the evil of this place.

It wasn't time to surrender, not even close.

I let go of the wheel and left Nate and Anica. I walked across the deck and quickly rotated the front cannon. I knew the group had earlier loaded the cannons in preparation for a fight. I flipped open the small box fixed to the deck at the base of the cannon. I retrieved one of

169

the precut fuses and the lighter. I jabbed the fuse in the small hole at the cannon's rear, opened the lighter, and ignited the fuse. It immediately began to spit sparks as the fire raced toward the pack of explosives.

"Heads down!" I shouted and dived for the area behind the foremast.

The fire disappeared in the hole. There was a long, agonizing moment of silence, making me believe the shot was a dud. When I peeked around the edge of the mast, I saw fire cough from the barrel, and instantly following was an impressive explosion.

I couldn't see the cannonball within the tower of smoke and flames. However, we all heard the solid chunk of steel smash into the wall. The hit blew apart the entire wall section with such a fierce grip on the ship's bow.

Suddenly the ship began righting itself as the bow broke from the cavern and found daylight. The Good Ship was free as we were finally starting our voyage. We were also now running for our lives.

"Brilliant move, Annabelle," Anica shouted.

Nate quickly stood from his covered position and retook the wheel. Anica, Jacob, and Cody joined me at the base of the mainmast. I followed their instructions as the four of us worked in total focus to get the sails up, catch the wind, and race us to our primary destination.

It took several minutes before the massive white sails were rising toward the top of the three masts. It was a few heart-stopping seconds after that when the wind rebounded off the cliff face and finally found the beautifully made sails.

I was almost thrown off my feet when the wind grabbed us. The ship jolted forward and quickly cut its way across the gently swelling waves.

As the ship made a steady turn to the port side, I glanced over my shoulder and saw the nearly equally sized green ship begin pursuit. The Jade Army had been blasting away at the cliffs on the southwest side of the island. Fortunately, the distance was going to give us a bit of a lead. We had a few tricks up our sleeves. We wanted a fight because Nate and I had devised a plan. This plan had to work because I didn't think I'd allow myself to sail through the gateway unless the plan worked out perfectly.

I didn't know how long ago the Jade Army had constructed their ship. It had once been an intimidating creation that demanded fear and respect.

We had built ours bigger, stronger, and faster.

I was well aware that their cannons could turn this ship into Swiss cheese should we allow them the opportunity. However, the timeframe in which our plan went into effect was going to be a small window of opportunity. We would be at a momentary standstill. I was sure that during this time, the Good Ship would take on major damage.

The bow rose and fell as the ship cut through the waves. The sails had taken full advantage of the wind and pushed us hard and fast. We could have easily outrun the Jade Army if the desire was there.

I looked out to the horizon, squinting from the sun. I searched for the strange gateway of light that pulled us from our world and thrust us somewhere beyond all of our imaginations. I knew that the gateway was still quite a distance away if it was even there at all. I did have faith in Nate's calculations. I knew that if he said the gateway would be in a particular position at a specific time, then I could very well bet on it.

"Nate, let Anica take the wheel. You and I have to prepare the cannons for the next step," I said.

"Right," Nate said. He gave Anica quick instructions on our heading and then joined me.

"So tell me that this stupid plan is going to work. Tell me it won't capsize both ships and kill us all," I said.

"Well, I can't make any promises like that. I do think it's a pretty good plan and has a huge potential for success. The only thing worrying me at this point is that if these hooks and cables will hold up. If the cables snap under the tension, there could be some serious injuries if these cables spring back at our families on the other ship or us," Nate said.

"Yeah, believe me when I tell you that I've thought of that over and over. All right, let's set these things in position and wait for our opportunity," I said.

A couple of kids from below deck appeared and offered to help with whatever needed doing. We gave them the vital chore of coiling steel cables. When the time comes, the cables will need to unwind without the chance of snagging on themselves or anything else.

Nate and I packed the brilliantly engineered cannons with explosive powder, followed by packing wads to fit around the hooks' back ends for a tight fit. This way, all the explosive force stayed behind the hooks and not escaping around the load. We made sure the cables were securely fastened and then rammed the hooks down the cannon barrels. It was a process requiring the greatest attention.

When the task of setting up the three stern cannons was complete, Nate and I triple-checked each steel cable and the newly constructed hooks. We walked to the railing at the stern and gave a long inspection of the steel plates bolted to the hull. I could see the three cable ends securely fastened to each plate. I hoped everything was going to hold up under extreme pressure. We looked at each other and nodded approval that everything was as good as it was going to get.

"Do you realize that we're going to have to fire these far in advance before we reach the gateway? If the hooks don't get a bite on their ship, or if there isn't enough explosive powder to propel the hooks that far, we'll need to retry or come up with another plan in a hurry," Nate said.

"Have you always been a person who looks toward the negative side of things?" I asked.

"I'm just saying. I would hate to see all this hard work come up with zero results. I know we all want it to work out, but I hate to think of the possibility that it doesn't."

"It'll work. There won't be a need for a plan B. You'll see," I said confidently.

As Nate and I made our way to the bow, Nate's words, unfortunately, began working into my brain. I was now starting to ask myself, *what if?*

Nate cupped his hands around his eyes at the ship's bow and studied the shimmering blue horizon.

"I think I see it. I think I see the gateway. I think I see the light," Nate said excitedly.

I mimicked Nate's motions by shielding the sun from my eyes and searched the distance. If it was there, I certainly couldn't see it. It must have still been several nautical miles away. I wanted to trust his eagle eye and judgment.

There was an echoing blast behind us. We all turned to see that the Jade Army had rotated their deck cannons forward. They were now making a desperate attempt to hit us with a cannonball and somehow disable us. None of the shots found us but fell short with a small splash in our wake.

"The Jade Army realizes we're going to escape. They're trying everything possible to stop us," Anica said from the captain's wheel.

"Yeah, it'll be amusing to see the expression on their faces when we drop our sails and let them catch up. I kind of wish I had a camera to capture the moment," I added.

"When you were with Graur at the other island, are you sure you heard Roland say that the entire army was going to be on the ship?" Nate asked, a little worried.

"I'm positive. Unless the Jade Army changed plans since we left, but I don't think so. Roland said he wanted the entire army to see the destruction of those who have opposed them for so long. I think all of them are on board. Your family, my family, and everyone else's family should be there."

Nate studied the horizon again. After a minute, he pointed to something in the distance and smiled.

I saw it too. Ahead of us was a faint glow of multicolored lights dancing on the horizon. We found the gateway.

"Well, I guess it's time to drop the sails and start the fun," I said.

23

The Last Stand

Anica ordered the sails to fall, and just like that, the ship was slowing its momentum. In no time flat, we were like a dead fish in the water.

There were now dozens of us on the ship's deck. We all watched with nervous eyes as the Jade Army drew too close for comfort. It was insane to think this was supposed to be a good plan.

A cannon fired again. The shot was much closer this time. I was well aware that the next shot or two was going to find a wooden target. I hoped my plan wasn't going to get someone killed.

"They're pulling up fast. We need to raise the sails and get going again," Anica shouted from the wheel.

We did. The wind resisted for a few unsettling moments as the sails only fluttered but wouldn't grab the wind.

Four of us adjusted the boom until we caught the direction of the wind, and then the sails billowed out. We were on the run again. This time the Jade Army was now within easy reach of us.

Cannons roared again. A section of the port side railing disintegrated into a shower of splinters as a cannonball found our ship. It wasn't going to take long before those shots were tearing large holes in our hull and flooding the entire ship with water.

When the Jade Army ship began moving up on our port side, I finally found the nerve to take a long look at the angry crowd. I was trying to find two particular faces I knew well. There were so many that it was nearly impossible to focus on a single person for more than a second. I thought I spotted my brother but quickly lost him in the wave of bodies. I couldn't have been positive, but I was pretty sure that it was him. If Brad were on the green ship, it would make sense for my father to be there.

"We should fire now!" Nate screamed.

"No! They need to be closer. Find your positions!" Anica said.

For the briefest of moments, I thought maybe Anica was afraid to fire the cannons. I thought she could very well be terrified of the plan being a complete failure. An instant later, I realized Anica wasn't afraid. I understood that she was right. She knew the Jade Army had to be even closer to give the hooks a chance at grabbing the other ship.

Nate, Jacob, and I found our positions beside the stern cannons. We had three shots to grab hold of the other ship. I knew one hook wouldn't do it. I was pretty sure even two certainly wouldn't be enough. It had to be all three hooks. If any of the shots were to fall short or not find a piece of the ship to bite into, then our efforts would most likely be for nothing.

The Jade Army was now a stone throw away. The giant ship was pulling alongside us, but we still had a small lead on them.

A mob of crewmembers moved around their ship. The cannons were being reloaded and situated for a direct hit. I saw angry, tormented faces desiring to see our ship blown in half and sunk. The power Simora has on these once peaceful people was overwhelming. I wanted to see their will crumble, which would equally shatter Simora's vengeful control over them. At least I hoped so.

The truth is, all of us can only speculate on the outcome when we travel back through the gateway. We weren't even sure a ship would be allowed to sail through in the opposite direction. As far as we knew, our ship could hit the gateway like it was an impenetrable concrete barrier and crumble our beautiful boat to pieces. Everything seems to be a guess at this point.

Anica turned her sight from the distant glowing gateway. She looked at each of us and then to the green ship that was uncomfortably close.

Anica's arm shot out. Her fist raised toward the opposing vessel, and she screamed, "Fire!"

I flicked the lighter. The wind immediately killed the flame. I tried again, this time cupping my other hand around the fire. It took four tries before the fuse grabbed the flame. It began spitting orange embers as the fire ran a fast-paced race for the small hole.

I backed away from the cannon. I saw Nate and Jacob had similar problems but also overcame them. Each of us watched with hope that the hooks would find a solid hold on the other boat.

My cannon was the first to thunder. The end of the barrel turned into a billowing inferno. I didn't see the hook take flight but realized that it was on its way because the steel cable was quickly unraveling from its coil.

I then saw the well-crafted hook soar like a beautiful eagle across the small span of blue water and then collapsed with a clang onto the deck of the other ship. A dozen bodies had dodged out of the path of the falling object.

Nate's cannon fired, and Jacob's cannon rumbled a split second later. The other two hooks were quickly on the way.

As we pulled farther ahead, my hook ran across the deck, momentarily hung up on the base of a cannon, tore loose, and eventually found purchase at the lowest part of the mainmast. One by one, each hook sank sharp points into a strong length of wood.

The Jade Army didn't have enough time to figure out what to do before the slack in the cables pulled tight as our ship gained more of a lead.

The Good Ship jolted back. The majority of us slid off our feet. The other ship surged forward from our massive pull. I saw most of the army stumble and fall. Thankfully, no one went overboard.

The cables groaned in protest as the tension was almost more than they could withstand. Despite the enormous weight, the cables did their duty.

"It's working! It's working!" Anica called to us.

She had spoken too soon.

With a combined total of materials and crewmembers, I couldn't have even closely guessed the total amount these ships weighed. I knew the numbers had to be incredibly high. We should have known earlier that three cables certainly wouldn't be enough.

The cable I had fired was now under so much tension that the braided steel strands started to break.

We all realized at the same moment that it wasn't because the cables couldn't withstand towing the other ship. It was because the Jade Army had made a course correction. They were now desperately trying to pull away from us.

They must have figured out that the only way to break the grip was not to spend time trying to free the hooks but to use their ship's weight against us. By pulling away from us, they knew the resistance would be too great for the cables.

"Nate, load this cannon," I said, as I quickly calculated a dozen different things at once.

"Load it for what? We don't have any more hooks, Annabelle," Nate said.

"Do it. Load it with a steel ball and make it super quick."

If one of the cables broke, the others would soon follow. I had to make the shot count, or all of this would be for nothing. If I missed, the Jade Army would be free of our hold, and I would forever lose my father and brother. I couldn't let that happen, not for anything in the world.

Nate finished packing the powder and began loading the ball. I set the extremely short fuse and retrieved the lighter from my pocket. Once I had my aim set, I knew I needed the fuse to light on the first try. If I stumbled with the fuse like I did while trying to shoot the hook, my sights would be off, and the shot would be a definite miss.

"Okay, it's ready to go," Nate said.

"Hurry and help me rotate the cannon to the left."

Although Jacob had no idea of where my crazy plan was going, he ran over to us and helped shift the cannon in place.

"Good. Now we need to lower the back end. I need the shot to go a little high."

The three of us put our weight down on the heavy tree trunk, which now acted as a cannon. When I had the right setting, I locked the cannon in place.

"Are you sure you know what you're doing?" Nate asked.

179

"I think I've figured out the special skill I can use to contribute to the cause. I have a freakishly great sense of accuracy. I think it's something I had when I was born. I think it's the one way I can help," I said while waiting patiently for my shot.

Anica made a slight course correction as she steered ahead of the other ship. She was doing a fantastic job of keeping our hold on the other boat while I waited to pull a rabbit from my magic hat.

Both of the ships hit a big swell. We went up the wave, and the bow crashed down and then up again. The ocean had seemed relatively calm only moments ago but was now greatly unsettled. I caught a glimpse of the sky. It had mostly darkened in such a short time. The center of the blackening sky hovered over the island my friends once considered their home.

If the ocean grew more agitated, my shot would be impossible.

Truthfully, I wasn't entirely sure I could deliver what I hoped. My particular skill has limits, just like everything else. Finding the trajectory and timing by throwing something with precise accuracy isn't a challenging task for me. I can knock a soda can off a fence post at thirty yards by calculating everything in a second flat. Throwing a rock at a stationary can is one thing. Now I have to calculate the shot at a moving target, but I also have to factor in the swells of the ocean and the ever-changing distance of the other ship as they desperately tried to break free. Not to forget, I have no idea the weight of the steel ball or how much powder Nate packed behind it. Luck has to be on my side to make this shot even close.

I could feel dozens of eyes on me.

The Jade Army fired another round. It took out a railing section before the cannonball violently skipped across the deck and into the water.

I glanced to my left and saw a rising wave.

Our ship ran up the wave. The Jade Army followed.

Our ship hit the crest of the wave and began to drop. I quickly rechecked my aim.

Just before the other ship found the peak of the wave, I lit the fuse.

I quickly backed away and covered my ears, but my eyes were wide and unblinking.

The Jade Army's ship momentarily paused at the peak of the wave, and just before gravity pulled them back down, the cannon viciously roared.

A torrent of fire spewed from the end of the barrel. I briefly saw a large gray molded chunk of steel take flight. The cannonball quickly raced across the open water. I saw dozens of the army members take cover when they realized that this shot wasn't another hook.

The shot miraculously found its target.

The cannonball struck the mainmast just below the boom. The shot took out more than half the diameter of the mast and devastated the remaining wood. I almost told Nate to reload the cannon for another shot but held my tongue as I heard the splintering wood give way from the offset of the mast's weight.

The fall of the giant mast happened right before our eyes as the wind forced the mast forward and down. A sea of bodies moved toward the very edges of the ship. The entire mainmast, riggings, and the sail came crashing down on the crew.

A wave of cheers erupted from our ship.

I didn't have the enthusiasm to cheer. I felt a cold, unsettling grumble in the pit of my stomach. All I could think of was the number of people hurt during the collapse of all that material.

The cheer from my fellow shipmates was short-lived.

A moment later, something powerful and sinister awoke on the island.

We always believed that it was impossible, but Simora forced her way into the daylight.

We were stealing Simora's army, and she was coming to reclaim them.

<u>24</u>

Lothlora, the Ancient One

At about the time Simora's rage began to build, something just as powerful awoke from a long sleep.

The dim lights in the depth of the lake grew ever brighter. Something ancient began churning on the murky bottom. The once crystal clear water took on a muddy coloration as the creation in the deep started to rise.

We saw and heard something tearing through the massive trees, splintering them as if they were simply toothpicks in the sand. We couldn't see the thing itself, but the presence of something great and sinister was known.

We were quite a distance from the island now, but I was sure that the creature had originated from the area we knew to be Simora's domain. I wondered if maybe she has a psychic link to each member of the Jade Army. Perhaps she was now well aware of the trouble facing her pitiful army.

The entire crew of the Jade Army stopped what they were doing and also watched the distance. I figured they knew Simora was trying to stop us from reaching the gateway. Maybe she was even coming to destroy us.

"I think this new development isn't good," Anica said as she glanced over her shoulder.

Now that the Jade Army's ship no longer has the power to break away from us, Anica could redirect our path for a straight shot at the gateway. We were only two nautical miles away, but for some reason, I didn't think that was close enough.

"It has to be Simora. I can't think of anything else it can be," Jacob said.

We all watched the treetops tumble as the thing crashed across the island in a direct line toward the beach.

"That can't be possible. I've never known Simora able to come out in the daytime," Nate said.

I said, "What if she fully understands what's going on? What if she knows we're going to travel through the gateway and take her entire army with us? If we take everyone back through the gateway, she knows her power will break. If she understands that she's going to die, wouldn't that make her far more powerful for a short period to save her own life? When something wants to live so badly, it would be able to do almost anything to ensure survival."

An enormous black creature divided the trees at the beach and rolled deep into the sand. Because of the distance and the creature's quick movement, I didn't think any of us knew what shape this thing had taken. There was an eruption of sand as it moved down the shoreline and into the ocean.

Whatever the thing was, it was coming fast.

"Is there anything we can do to go faster?" I asked Anica.

"If we lighten the load on the ship, then we might pick up a little more speed. But by the time we started throwing stuff overboard, that thing will be here. We have to hang on and take things as they come," she said.

"This is going to sound stupid, but I think we might need to reload the cannons," Jacob said.

I didn't think it would do much good against our pursuer. I raced anyway to one of the cannons at the stern and started loading one of the packets of explosives, following it with a steel ball. Nate and Jacob went to the other two cannons, and in moments, we were ready to fire.

"Wait until it shows itself. Don't panic and fire a shot into the water. We need a direct hit if we have a chance at stopping it," Nate suggested.

I thought of the battle at Simora's domain. She had come from the treetops in a black cloud. When she formed into the serpent, I had thrown a rock and hurt her. It was the same with the hunters. One hunter burned with a torch, and grouch trees and mischief attacked the others. They were only hurt after they transformed into a defined shape.

The anticipation was killing me. Not even my wildest dreams could have come up with any clue as to what this thing was.

A moment later, I realized that I was right because I would never have figured out what was going to come out of the water. It was simply water itself. It shot straight up like a waterfall in reverse. It defied gravity as thousands of gallons of water transformed. I could see the thing taking on defining shapes. It was a shape that looked eerily like a human, a massive tower of a human, but a human all the same. The head of the water structure dominated our ship's mainmast by at least two stories. The entire body moved beside our ship as we desperately tried to reach the gateway.

As the shifting completed, the thing's head turned down to us. Its eyes ignited a brilliant green.

I've seen those eyes before.

It *was* Simora.

She was different from the intimidating figure of the giant black serpent I first encountered. Now she had taken the form of something almost queen-like. I thought this appearance was how she once looked when she ruled the lands with her twin sister. She might have once been kind and perhaps even noble before greed overcame her.

As we watched in silent terror, Simora's features began rapidly changing. Her god-like appearance contorted and molded into something beyond imagination. She formed into a creature born from hate and the need for absolute power. She became a twisted, mangled creature somewhere between the appearance of a human and a deformed cave-dwelling troll. This transformation was Simora's real face.

Although it was only a light shade of blue water we were staring at, most of us looked away in disgust.

I looked toward the gateway and saw how very close we were.

I looked toward the other ship and saw Simora's army lowering their sight and bowing their bodies in either respect or fear.

I looked back at Simora.

I spotted movement from the corner of my eye as something approached from the southwest. It came at us just as Simora had. It rumbled through the water right for us.

"I don't think I can take anymore," Nate said. I was sure he also saw the movement coming from the island.

Simora's eyes flared, her mouth contorted in rage.

"Never! Never will you leave this place!" the thing roared at us in a voice very different from the raspy voice of the serpent.

Her arms rose high above her head. With probably all the force she could conjure, Simora slammed those columns of water down on us. The impact didn't feel like water but of flesh and bone.

I had the distinct feeling that a sledgehammer crashed into my entire body. All of us crumpled under the extreme weight of the water. Simora's arms shattered apart when they made contact with the ship, but a moment later, her nearly unlimited power drew up more water from the ocean and reconstructed her broken form. Her arms and fists then quickly dropped down on us again.

After the tremendous impact, I coughed out a mouthful of saltwater. I felt battered beyond my limit. I wasn't sure if I could take another assault.

It seems as if the gateway was so very close but also so very far away, as its rainbow of lights taunted us.

The foresail tore under the pressure of Simora's assault. The deck of the Good Ship had warped and splintered in places. A large section of the railing had broken away and dropped off into the depths of the ocean.

We once believed we could defeat the Jade Army. We thought we built the ship large enough and strong enough to win a war on the high seas. We couldn't have prepared for something of this magnitude. None of us had expected to face the relentless ruler of this strange land.

Lying on my back and waiting for another fierce strike, I heard the Jade Army cheer.

I looked at Nate and the others. We were all done in as the fight left us.

I felt myself slipping toward unconsciousness. Despite the eager pull to the realm of darkness, my mind

187

resisted the urge and pushed me back to the cruel world of reality. I opened my eyes and shifted my sight to the deck of the Jade Army ship. I saw happiness on their faces. Of course, this was false happiness as Simora had long ago stripped away every emotion except for hatred and greed.

What I was now feeling was one of these emotions. I suddenly felt a degree of hate course through my bones, my flesh, and blood. We had worked far too long and hard to lower our guns now. We wouldn't surrender at this point. We wouldn't give in until the last breath left our bodies.

I forced myself onto my hands and knees. I couldn't be sure of what the other thing was racing toward us, but I was pretty confident the war was no longer between just us. All I had to do was get us another minute.

As I stumbled by, I grabbed Nate by the collar and hauled him to his feet.

"Help me, quickly," I said.

I pulled Nate in beside me as I threw myself on the back end of the cannon. Our weight rotated the front end up and aimed directly at the center of Simora's watery creation. I worked the lighter from my pocket and made a quick prayer. Despite everything, the wet flint and wick sparked and ignited. The short fuse immediately caught the flame and raced into the hole.

Nate rolled off one side of the cannon. I rolled off the other side a few seconds before the cannon roared.

I knew the attempt was a ridiculous idea, but the cannonball did as I had hoped.

The shot caught Simora's left shoulder, disrupting the power holding everything together, and the entire arm broke apart in a massive ripple. Instead of the arm crashing down on us again, the water fell in heavy rain.

Her head turned, observing the damage done, and began reforming another arm.

I saw a wave to my right build like a relentless tsunami.

"Hit the deck!" I screamed to my friends.

Everyone saw and heard what was coming. The thing growing from the wave was far more dominating than Simora. What materialized out of that wave was a creation with the same appearance Simora first revealed to us.

I was sure that we were now getting our first look at the twin sister once long lost. I did not doubt that this was the sister who found sanctuary at the bottom of the lake. It was Lothlora, the sister with a good heart and an unmatched kindness once loved by all those she helped create so long ago.

Nate watched with amazement. While bouncing with excitement, he pointed to the rolling wave now resembling an elegant queen once forgotten.

He said, "I can't believe it, it's Lothlora! She's really real!"

Lothlora's eyes flared a magical green. Those eyes momentarily reminded me of Graur's eyes.

Simora's body turned to face her sister. I saw a look of genuine surprise. I knew the expression I saw after that was pure dread. Simora was truly afraid of her sister.

Our ships sailed on toward the gateway as the twin sisters converged after hundreds or even thousands of years apart. The two structures made up of simply seawater smashed into each other and blew apart in a rainstorm. Within seconds, the water began bubbling in two areas as the sisters reformed. I saw ship wreckage pulled up from the bottom of the ocean inside Simora as she finished rebuilding herself.

189

As Lothlora reconstructed her body, she unintentionally captured an orange giant squid. It swam in quick circles in her belly, unable to escape the magical formation. Lothlora's new body surpassed her original size. She became twice the height as well as twice the width of Simora.

"I think Lothlora is far more powerful than Simora," I excitedly told Nate.

"How do you figure that? She's been hiding away for a long time," he said.

"Exactly. Lothlora has stayed in a neutral position for so long that her energy never really diminished. Simora has worn herself down for so long by using the resources of her energy chasing us every day. Whatever power she's received from the people she's corrupted wasn't nearly enough to sustain her for very long. She's been dying for a long time," I said.

The streaming lights of the gateway danced in front of our ship. The rhythmic whump-whump-whump sounds of that beautiful doorway to another world called to us.

Lothlora had bought us the time we needed.

"Simora is fighting for her life to stop us. Lothlora is fighting to set us free. I think you're right, Nate. I think once we journey back through the gateway, everything Simora has stolen from us will be returned," I said with confidence.

A horrible thought entered my mind at that moment. If what I was saying was the truth, then that means all of us would return to the point in history in which we disappeared. That means that in a moment, Nate and I will no longer be together. Nate will magically transport back to a time when humanity has yet to know of a world war. The gateway would toss me back to a time when our country was beginning the Vietnam War, and hippies were running wild.

I stepped beside Nate and gently took his hand. Our eyes held each other for a long moment.

"Annabelle, whatever comes next, I want you to know that you're the best thing to ever happen to me," he said.

"I don't want to forget you. I don't want to forget any of you," I said as the children from below deck began coming up the steps one by one.

Behind us, the war between sisters raged on. I was sure I knew what the outcome would be. Whether the war was long or short, good always prevails.

Although our numbers were a third of the Jade Army's three hundred, the good had dominated and overcame the toughest of obstacles.

The fight had left the minds and hearts of the Jade Army. I didn't see an angry face among them. What I did see, what I believed to be, was a sense of hope. Their now peaceful eyes were watching the beautiful floating lights of the gateway. Maybe they were beginning to remember small pieces of themselves that were lost or stolen somewhere along the way.

"I won't forget any of you. I won't let myself forget the kindness and friendship each of you has shown me. I love each of you like a brother, sister, or a really, really close friend." I looked at Nate as I said the last words and winked.

Nate winked back and held my hand tighter.

When the bow of the ship pierced the gateway, I felt a warm peacefulness embrace me like the comforting arms of my mother. I felt a single tear spill down my cheek as the sadness of losing friends found the center of my heart.

191

"Thank you for giving me the greatest adventure of my life," I told Nate, as the brilliantly majestic light of the gateway took us to places unknown.

25

The Gateway Closes

My arm hair stood on end. I heard the hard buzzing like electricity running through wires. I couldn't see a thing except a flashing of excited light offering more colors than a rainbow.

I still felt Nate's hand in mine. He held on tight, dreading the light would tear us apart. I realize it's been over fifty years since the doorway of light ate up Nate. I couldn't imagine the terror he must be feeling of what was to come next.

I have only been gone a little under a month. Then again, that made me wonder. Was the time on the other side of the gateway running a different race? What I mean is, does time completely stop on the other side? None of the children had grown older. Maybe that's because of the magical powers of the twin sisters. The sun rose and fell each day on the island, so that must mean that time was still moving forward. Or maybe for each day on the island, it was an entire year in our world. I was confusing myself. I decided I would eventually find out when, if, we found other people.

The fingers of light broke from my skin, letting go with a bit of resistance. I looked at my hand, my sight traveling up Nate's arm to his gentle green eyes. He was smiling, a smile wider and more genuine than any before. He instantly knew we were free. We were free of the island and Simora's vicious hold over us. We were free of the gateway keeping us locked in a world that wasn't our home.

I looked behind us and saw the steel cables running from our stern to the web of light. The bow of the other ship finally broke through. A large green ship that wasn't there a moment before quickly began appearing foot by foot. Hundreds of confused faces searched the surroundings for answers. They watched each other, and they watched us. They then searched the vast blue water for something to make sense.

The hate and the anger covering their faces before entering the gateway were now gone. They appeared reborn. They were looking through cleared vision, no longer spellbound by a queen in an alternate universe. At that moment, I knew that the mind control Simora once had over them was now washed away like a bad dream.

The brightness of the gateway intensified as the rest of the Jade Army ship came through. Sparks flew like fireflies in a windstorm. A large and mighty hand came through, following two ships fighting to escape. The water of that hand rippled as the energy controlling it struggled to keep the form together. The power quickly faded as the hand began wrapping around the stern of the Jade Army's ship. The swirling ocean debris caught in the water started falling free, splashing into the ships' wake and returning to the ocean depths. The hand then came apart in a total collapse. Heavy drops of water hammered the ocean behind the ship.

The gateway flared an angry red. I was sure Simora realized her powers had no lasting effect in this world.

Even with all her evil and hatred, she couldn't stop us from sailing away from her sinister control.

I wondered then, would Simora cease to exist now that her crew of the Jade Army no longer fed her with their hatred? I remember when she held me in her dark nest. I remember being transfixed by her hypnotic eyes. I also remember feeling everything good and pure being pulled from me until nothing would remain except hate and greed. I was fortunate to get away without losing a bit of myself.

"Look," Nate shouted.

I saw it. The redness of the gateway made a smooth change to forest green and then pale blue. The pulsing of the light reminding me of a heartbeat slowing like a dying clock. Just like that, it blinked out of existence. Now only the ocean was seen where the gateway had been.

"Simora's gone. She's finished," one of the children said.

I prayed he was right. I would love nothing more than to think the world on the other side would be filled with peace from now on. I hoped Graur and all the other animals would no longer have to live in perpetual fear of a dark queen. Maybe Simora blinked out of existence just like the gateway. Maybe Lothlora, a queen of love and happiness, would take over the lands. I suppose I'll never know for sure.

I looked out at the ocean. I saw nothing but blue water and on top of that was a cloudless blue sky. There were no distinct silhouettes of islands or any other mass of land. We are now two ships sitting in a vast emptiness. I couldn't even be entirely sure which direction we were heading. One ship was crippled, and the other barely hanging on.

I had something important I needed to know. I moved to the stern railing and looked out at the faces of the Jade Army. Of course, now they were the only people who had gone missing from our world decades before. They asked each other their names and tried to understand why they were on a pirate ship in the middle of the ocean. It seemed to me that they had returned to the lives they once knew before Simora stripped the decency from them.

"Brad! Dad!" I called at the top of my voice.

There were so many faces. They moved around so much it was hard to find the two people I hoped were there. I didn't know what I would do if my father and Brad were left behind, stuck in a world where a doorway of light was now and possibly forever closed.

I then heard the voice of a child. It was soft and barely audible among the chatter of the crew. That voice and another grew louder. Those voices called my name. It had to be my family because no one of the Jade Army knew who I was.

The crowd parted as two people struggled to get through. My heart leaped into my throat when I saw them break through and reach the bow. They were incredibly filthy. Their clothes were torn and covered in dirt. Their hair shaggy and oily from lack of being washed, and my father had a thick beard, but they were the most beautiful sight on earth.

A smile stretching from ear to ear found my face. My father and Brad made it through all right. My family has now returned to me. They looked worn down from doing duties they would never recall, but they were undoubtedly back.

"Are you all right?" my father asked.

"Great," I said. "I'm just great."

Nate and the others started lowering our sails. Our momentum slowed, and the green ship slid up beside us. I leaped the short distance between ships and into my father's outstretched arms. Brad wrapped his arms around us. I was sure Heaven must be just like this. Love, pure love, for each other is all we needed.

"You have no idea how much I've missed the two of you," I told them.

I kissed my father and brother. My heartbeat quickened. I hadn't felt this sort of happiness since long before my mother passed away.

Brad said, "There's one thing I've got to know. What the heck is going on?"

I wondered what they would think when I had a chance to spill everything out. Would they believe me? Would any member of the Jade Army believe a spun tale about another world, an evil serpent with hypnotic eyes, and about time having no meaning? It would be hard for most of them to swallow. I figured two large ships in the middle of the ocean would help them grasp the truth. I have no doubt they would all remember a time when their boat was snatched up by a doorway of light and seeing that same doorway spit them back out.

I said, "There will be plenty of time to catch up on current events. We have more important things to figure out right now. When we left the light, we came out to a place that could be anywhere on earth. We're not sure at all which direction we should be sailing. The mainsail of this ship is busted, thanks to me. The Good Ship is sluggish trying to tow something this big. We can't fit everyone on one ship, so we're going to have to keep limping along until we spot another vessel and get help."

197

My father nodded as if this immediately made sense. My father is always a man to take charge, and now he did as I expected.

"Let's go over to the other ship. First, I want to meet your friends. Then we'll figure out where we go from here," my father said.

We leaped to the other ship. I began introducing my father and brother to the group. When we got to Nate, I said, "This would be Nate. He's older than dirt but looks good for his extreme old age. Nate is the first person I met. I'd say he's been a best friend to me during my time on the island."

My father shook Nate's hand and said, "Thank you for looking out for my little girl. I suppose I owe you a great debt."

"It was my pleasure. I will tell you that Annabelle and I kissed. Well, she kissed me more than I kissed her," Nate said.

My face bloomed red. I didn't know if Nate said this to embarrass me or because it was customary during his time in the 1800s to tell adults this news.

I elbowed him in the ribs and then gave him a disapproving glare. "Not appropriate," I said from the corner of my mouth.

"Well, then I guess you'll have to marry her once we find land and a preacher to do the ceremony," my father said and winked. "First things first, we've got to figure our position on this spinning blue marble called Earth. Then we have to pick a direction giving us the best chance at finding either land or a ship crossing."

Groups of the Jade Army crossed over to our ship until the deck was full.

I started to say something to Nate, but his eyes locked on something over my shoulder. I turned and looked.

Roland, Nate's identical twin, was walking toward us. Roland was smiling, and tears began spilling down his cheeks. I looked at Nate. He started crying as well. Without a single word, the brothers embraced. They cried and laughed and then pulled back and looked each other over.

I knew the feeling. I was glad to have my father and brother back in my life. I could only imagine how Nate felt, as it has been countless decades since he has last seen his twin brother.

"Where's—" Roland began, then Max threw himself against his brother in a hug.

"Boys! Boys!" a woman called out.

The crowd parted as two people slipped through. The three sons were the spitting image of their father. They took in the sight of their sons. More tears came, and the five of them wrapped around each other.

I looked around. Many people were rejoining with long-lost family members. I thought of the terror only a blink ago as we tried to get away from an evil governess, but now only happiness filled the crowd.

After giving the families a bit of time to reconnect, my father went onto the upper deck beside the ship's wheel and let out a stout whistle. The crowd hushed and turned toward him.

"My name is Tom Cross. I'm thrilled everyone is reconnecting with family. It's certainly a time for celebration. However, we're in quite a pickle because we are lost in the middle of the ocean. One ship is nearly crippled, and the other can't hold all of us. First, we need to figure out to the best of our knowledge where that thing of light put us. I will tell you that my family and I were heading for the western coast of South Africa when we

199

got sucked in. By a show of hands, was anyone not on the Atlantic when they got pulled into that other world?"

No one raised their hand.

"Good. I guess that narrows it down a bit," my father said.

An older man with a British accent said, "We were heading the other direction toward New York City."

Everyone else started calling out their destination before the light took them. It all concluded that the gateway wasn't something appearing around many oceans but staying close to where we currently are.

"Well, now I suspect we're getting somewhere. We've got a better chance at pinpointing our location and figuring out where to go from here," my father said. "Do you have a compass on board?"

One of the kids came forward and handed the only compass to my father. Another boy from our group offered my father a tattered atlas that looked fifty years old.

"Good. Thank you," my father said.

My father got to work as the chatter of people started again. He went around the ship and asked people to point out on the map where they figured they went missing. Some people couldn't recall because it had been so long ago. My father worked the figures the best he could.

After nearly an hour, my father whistled again to get everyone's attention. "I've spoken to most of you trying to understand where exactly we could be. By the information you've all shared with me, I've determined that we're somewhere right about here," he said as he pointed to a spot on the map. "About eight hundred and fifty miles from the eastern coast of the United States."

A wave of groans flowed through the crowd. They all knew that with a busted ship, it might as well have been Mars we were aiming to reach.

"We have a couple of options here. There's a cluster of islands a bit closer to the south. However, I honestly don't know if people are there. There's something else we can do. We could unhook the green ship and sail this one for the U.S. We could send the coast guard or someone out to get the rest of you. Our third option is that we can limp both ships to the States. I'm not deciding because we all have a vote. By a show of hands, who thinks we should head for the islands?"

There were a few hands, but not many.

"Who believes we should leave the damaged ship with selected crew members and sail this ship to find help?"

A quarter of the hands went up.

"And finally, who thinks we're all in this together, and we should continue traveling in one group?"

This final question brought up the majority of the hands.

"All right, it's settled then. First, we'll have to work on securing more cables to the other ship. We'll also need to do an inventory of all the food, water, and other supplies we have on both ships."

My father and several other men began assigning tasks. In a short amount of time, hundreds of people were moving around taking care of business. For the first time, the Jade Army and the base camp children worked together to reach the same goal. We all wanted to get home, even the ones who would return to a world far different from the one they left.

Nate and I volunteered to secure more cables between ships. Being that I'm the one who damaged the other ship's mainmast, I felt obligated to see to it that our ships stayed together for either a good or bad outcome.

After working ourselves into rope harnesses, Nate and I dangled over the ship's stern. The work was difficult as we moved heavy steel plates and bolted them to the ship. Three people lowered the cables to us, and we fastened them to the eye hooks on the steel plates. We still needed to fix the other end of the cables to the Jade Army ship, and we were ready to set sail again.

Anica appeared from the lower deck. She approached Nate, my father, and me. "Well, here's the rundown of things. The Jade Army ship wasn't well equipped with food, water, or other supplies. They were probably planning on hitting our ship, sinking it, and heading back to their island. We fully stocked our ship before leaving. The problem is that we weren't expecting to have three hundred more mouths to feed. We'll have to be very careful about how much every person gets each day. The supplies we have on hand should last us thirteen days. If we cut rations a little more, we could stretch it to sixteen days. Cutting food and water any more than that will make people very sick, and most will likely start to die."

My father said, "Let's all at least pray for some rain we can collect. Well, then I guess time is pressing on us. We've got to get the sails back up and on our way."

For most people here, for the first time in years, time is now a crucial thing.

26

Sabotage

"Let's hope the cables hold," Nate said as we worked to raise the sails of the Good Ship.

"They'll hold. Trust me," I told Nate.

There was a strong wind coming from the east. The sails fluttered as we strained to raise the massive canvas. We shifted the boom just right, and the wind bit deeply into the sails. The Good Ship shot forward hard enough that I nearly came off my feet. There was an immediate pause as the cables became strained, offering a hard tug on the other ship. I heard the cables groan under pressure, but as I told Nate, they held.

"Well, that's a good sign," my father said, as our ships steadily cut through the water and picked up speed.

"If a strange thing of light appears in front of us, I'm jumping overboard," I told those around me. "I think I'd rather be shark bait before I go back to that place."

Many agreed with me.

I kept watching our momentum pick up speed. I glanced back every so often to see the other ship smoothly following in our wake.

Nate and I locked eyes. We smiled at each other, and then his hand was in mine. It felt good, and it felt right for our hands to be together just like this.

Someone's arms wrapped around my waist. Brad's face was there at my side. He watched the horizon with a little smile at the corners of his mouth.

"We're going to find it, aren't we? The land, I mean. Will we all make it home?" Brad asked.

I patted Brad's arms. We've had our differences over the years as he was a bratty little brother, and I was a know-it-all big sister. We knew this about each other, and it was all right. We love each other regardless of our petty differences. We're family, and our bond is unbreakable.

"I do believe so. We've got the intelligence and the motivation to see this to the very end. I can't think of a single person on these ships who doesn't want to find a place called home," I told him.

Nate leaned in and said, "I don't know if you heard me earlier talking to your father, but my name is Nate."

Brad smiled. "I heard. You kissed my sister."

"Again, it was more her kissing me. Your father said we'll have to be married when we get back, so I guess that will make you my brother-in-law."

I elbowed Nate again.

"Cool. I've always wanted a big brother," Brad said.

I rolled my eyes. "I'm only thirteen. I'm not getting married for a long, long time."

"Well, as you've said, I'm older than dirt, so for me, it's going to be now or never," he said and winked.

"You know, for being that old, I would have thought you'd be a lot smarter," I said.

Because the blazing sun was cruel during the daytime, most of the crew stayed below in the shade. It was still hot down there, but dehydration didn't hit near as bad. We needed to conserve our drinking water as long as possible. Many of us slept on the deck under brilliant stars winking at us from a thousand light-years away. The second night as I stared at those glowing dots trying to let my mind slip into rest, I wondered if there was a thirteen-year-old girl on a planet out there staring right back at me.

The Good Ship fought on, reaching for a destination that seemed somewhere beyond the edge of the universe.

We played made-up games for entertainment. We all slept a lot. We hung ropes from the mast and swung out over the ocean as if we were Tarzan. We also talked until most of us had nothing left to say. We did anything and everything possible to try to keep our minds from going mad.

I only had my father and Brad to speak with before the doorway of light swallowed us. Now there were hundreds of people and thousands of stories to hear. I enjoyed talking with those who were on the island before the turn of the century. It was fun telling them about automobiles, televisions, and airplanes. Most of them were in disbelief until the fifth day when an aircraft cut a white streak across the pale blue sky.

My father said it looked like we are now on the right path. We followed that plane's direction until it got so far away that the blue sky eventually ate it.

Nate and I were below in the galley on the eleventh day, making an afternoon snack of apple slices, when someone toward the stern screamed. It was a high-pitched scream that only a girl can make. We ran to that sound, not knowing what to expect. Sitting on the floor was a bomb. I recognized it the second I saw it because we used the same explosives to blow down the cavern wall.

"Somebody—somebody put that—" a girl I didn't know was saying.

"Oh, my God," I said as I moved toward it.

We weren't going to have time to pull the fuse from the explosives as the flame disappeared in the bundle. Nate grabbed the girl and pushed her toward the doorway. She tripped and went down. Nate tackled me, and painfully I went down as well.

The world ended just then in a deafening blast, shocking my ears to dead silence and kicking me like an angry mule. Fire rushed around us, and I felt the heat eat my skin. I was well aware that I would see a brilliant path leading to Heaven in the next second. Instead, the heat of the flames doused with cool Atlantic water. There was suddenly a hard tug on my legs. I thought Nate was trying to pull me somewhere. The explosion had created a ragged hole, and the concussion of the blast formed a sucking pocket of air beneath the ship. I didn't have enough body weight to fight its pull.

I searched for a hold on something. A hand seized my own as my body sank, and my head went underwater. Through stinging saltwater eyes, I saw Nate at the edge. He was crouched, trying to keep himself from being pulled down as well. He was shouting something, but my shocked ears were even deaf to the rush of water around me. I tried kicking, but the smooth flow of water beneath the ship wouldn't let go. Just like that, our hands broke apart. Nate became a blurred figure as I sank. The gliding rows of wood quickly replaced the sight of him as the ship passed overhead.

Here and now has become the ending to my story. Death has now become a sure thing. I was going to drown after everything that's happened to me since going through the doorway. My lungs hitched as the trapped air tried to break free. I almost let it go, but then the suction opened its death grip. The pocket of air forced down from the explosion began rising and taking me with it.

My head broke the surface. I pulled in a welcoming breath of air. I had enough time to take a few more breaths before I heard the rush of water shoved aside. I turned my head and realized I was about to be run down by a large green ship. It showed no signs of stopping because it couldn't. Faces peered over the railing. They must have been wondering how on earth I was suddenly in the water about to have my brains knocked out by their ship.

I had no time to swim to either side. My only chance was to dive. I drew in a deep breath and rotated my body as I kicked hard for the ocean depths. I must have gotten ten feet down when I felt the hard shove of water moving out of the way from the bow of the ship. Something bit at my feet, violently spinning my body so that I was no longer going down but parallel with the surface of the water. The hull of the ship was grabbing at me. My feet had hit, then my back, and then chest and face as I spun through the water. The water kept pushing me up as the ship battered me back down. I nearly blacked out, but I knew if I did, I would never wake up again. I didn't figure the torment would ever end, but then the stern of the ship spit me out.

I thankfully took in air. At the stern of the Jade Army ship, someone threw a white life preserver overboard. I didn't have much strength, but I knew I had to get it to save my own life. My paddling was weak, but after a few minutes, I reached it, worked my arms through the hole, and then let my muscles relax.

I nearly fell asleep due to exhaustion when someone called out. It was two voices I knew well. One was my father, and the other was Nate. I looked up to see a small rescue boat making its way to me.

"You're either the luckiest person I've ever met, or Heaven just isn't ready for you yet," Nate said when the boat stopped beside me.

I heard what he said, but barely. My ears were still fiercely ringing from the explosion.

"What does it matter anymore? Why are we continuing to fight to live? The Good Ship now has a big hole in it, and soon it'll be at the bottom of the ocean. The Jade Army ship is busted, and there's no way all the people will fit onboard," I told them.

"That doesn't sound like the Annabelle I know," my father said. He leaned over the side, hooked my arms, and pulled me from the water.

Nate said, "You sometimes have too little faith in a bunch of kids. Yes, the explosion opened a hole in the boat, but the crew is already getting a patch job done. Others are bailing out the water coming in. In case you're worried, it won't happen again. We've caught the saboteur. It was a boy from the Jade Army. He has no family aboard either ship to help him through this adjustment. So I guess it's harder for him to leave something he's known for so long. For the sake of safety, I think it would be best for the majority of the Jade Army to stay on board their ship. Of course, your family and mine would probably be all right to stay on the Good Ship."

I thought of Nate's twin brother, Roland, who was the leader of the Jade Army. If someone wanted to get back to the island, I figured it would be him, but I said nothing.

"I want to see the saboteur when we get back to the ship," I told them.

Even though I was exhausted, I managed to climb the rope ladder to the main deck. I received a lot of smiles and calls of being glad I was all right. Yes, I was all right, but I was also full-on mad.

"Where are you keeping him?" I asked Nate.

"He's in one of the rooms by the galley."

When I reached the bottom step, Nate pointed to a door down the corridor. When I went inside, I found a boy about a year younger than me sitting on the floor. His hands tied behind his back, and his eyes on the wooden floor. Tears were in his eyes. I saw torture in his face I've never seen in anyone before. If fury hadn't consumed me, then I might have felt pity for him.

I crouched next to his outstretched legs. He still couldn't meet my eyes.

"What's your name?" I asked as I swept wet hair from my face.

He sniffed and shook his head as if the question made no sense.

"You have a name. What is it?"

"Dawson," he said and then sniffed again.

"Well, Dawson, I'm not entirely sure why it is you're crying. It was the two of us plus several other kids who were nearly blown to tiny pieces by those explosives you set. I was pulled through the hole in the ship and almost drowned. Is that what you wanted? Were you planning on killing people?"

He shook his head a little bit.

I slammed my fist on the floor and shouted, "Look at me!"

His eyes snapped up in terror and locked on mine. They were dark eyes, almost black. I saw a lingering cruelness in them that may have remained a part of him since coming back through the gateway. Perhaps he's always had it. I didn't know.

I briefly wondered if a little part of Simora was still in each of the people from the Jade Army. Did a bit of evil still exist in my father and brother?

Nate's hand found my shoulder, and he squeezed a little. That touch told me to calm down. It said to me that the kid couldn't help doing what he had done. I didn't care how Nate felt.

I slapped the kid hard across the left cheek, and he looked at me in shocked amazement. His tears came faster. I began crying, too. There were overwhelming moments from my time on the island I had bottled up. This moment is where my emotions were uncorked, and all of that fear, sadness, and even loneliness came flooding out. I leaned in. He shied away, maybe thinking I was going to hit him again. Instead, I wrapped my arms around him in a fierce hug, and we cried on each other's shoulders.

"When we get back, it's going to be all right. You'll see," I said through sobs.

I didn't hate this kid or any of the others from the Jade Army. I hated the situation we've all been through and not knowing if we'd find a happy ending to it.

Call it whatever you want, luck, or even divine intervention, but I heard a lot of noise coming from the main deck.

"Hey, hey, everyone down below, you need to come up here and see this!" someone shouted down the stairs.

We couldn't resist his invitation. A mob of people crowded in the corridor, and one by one, we worked our way to the deck. The sun was blazing, and I shielded my eyes until they adjusted to the light. The crowd was thick, and it took me a few minutes to work my way to the bow. Nate was behind me. We reached the railing and studied the stretch of water in front of us. It was there on the horizon, moving at us with a hurried pace. One of the kids had the pair of binoculars we kept at the ship's wheel. I snatched them from her hands. As I studied the distant object, I realized it wasn't a mirage or anything caused by delirium.

"It's a ship!" I told them.

The group came alive with cheers and whistles.

I saw it then as the sun lit up what was on the bow of that ship.

"It's the U.S. Coast Guard!" I screamed.

I jumped in Nate's arms. My father and brother were quickly beside us. We wrapped together with the joy of knowing that everything we'd hoped to accomplish since our daring escape would come true.

Some people laughed, some cried, and some did both as the Coast Guard's steel boat slipped in beside us. Our main deck was several stories higher, so we looked down over the railing at the men in uniforms. There was an almost comical look on their faces as they studied the ships.

"Is everyone all right?" one of the men asked us.

Yes, I thought, we're just fine.

The captain of the vessel leaned out the window. He held the radio mike and said, "This is Captain Kline to base. Ah, base, you're not going to believe what we found out here. I swear we must have gone through a doorway in time."

27

The Beginning of the End

"Grandma? Hey, Grandma?" Zoe called.

"In the kitchen, sweetie," I said.

"Oh, there you are. Um, grandpa said that in a little while, we'd make s'mores outside by the fire. Would it be all right if we could?" she asked with bright, wide eyes.

"Well, I suppose if grandpa said we should, then I guess we had better."

Zoe yipped with excitement and hopped in place for a moment. She then ran from the room, declaring to all that very soon we'd be enjoying graham cracker, chocolatey marshmallow treats.

There's simply no denying it. I'm now a woman long past my prime, and I've never had any delusions of that. You could say I've even come to enjoy life well after the half-century mark. My life has been long and wonderful, and I wouldn't give back a second of it.

I should probably catch you up on a few things. It's only fair since you followed along with me on one of my exciting journeys. I think you deserve to know about what happened after the Good Ship reached land.

News crews quickly caught wind of the story. They began arriving where our ships docked on the eastern shore. Within a day, I think we had news stations from every major city across the country. Soon after that, international media began arriving to take pictures of our ships. They all wanted to hear the fantastic story of four hundred people who long ago vanished from the face of the earth.

There were, of course, the non-believers who claimed the entire thing to be a well-crafted hoax. Although seeing that we had nothing to gain by telling such a story, most people worldwide began to believe that there really could be a place just beyond our realm of existence.

All I want to say to those with such closed minds is simple: if you let yourself begin to believe, then worlds will open before your eyes.

I suppose I should take back what I said before about none of us gaining from our worldwide attention. That would probably make the non-believers happy to hear. Yes, many of us made fortunes since our return. There have been hundreds or even thousands of paid interviews done over these many years.

The Good Ship and the Jade Army ship received international attention when we decided to auction them off. The proceeds dispersed among the four hundred of us. Since most of the group didn't have a nickel to their names, we all made out pretty well in the end. All in all, both ships sold to private collectors for a total of twenty-two million dollars. You might think that's quite a lot for a couple of battered ships, especially back in the 1960s, but remember that a large number of children in a parallel dimension built them.

As I expected, my father gave up the desire to transport ships from country to country. Thank God for that. He made a career change to being an accomplished writer. He spent more than two years corroborating with dozens of us. He had taken down many thoughts and stories from my friends. These were the people who remembered. Unfortunately, the members of the Jade Army were under an unsettling spell, recalling little after they gazed into the eyes of the serpent.

Although many people have published books on our explorations, none experienced the world beyond the gateway. Their stories seemed to lack authenticity.

Since a member of the four hundred wrote the book, it sat at the top of bestseller's lists for a groundbreaking twenty-eight weeks.

Although he made a fortune from the book, my father only kept enough to live a comfortable lifestyle. He set up trust funds for Brad and me, which we received when we reached legal age. The rest of his fortune was given to those who still had difficulty getting back on their feet after returning to a world that dramatically changed without them.

My father finally found a new love. After a little over a year of dating, he married her on the breathtaking beaches of Hawaii. My brother and I understand that she could never replace our mother, but I think she's pretty terrific all the same. My father is happy again, and that's all that matters.

Brad the Brat survived adolescence by the skin of his teeth. Even after we returned home, his devilish tricks and rowdy behavior hadn't lightened up in the least. However, Brad's attitude completely flipped after high school. He began volunteering at many homeless shelters. Even when he attended Harvard with grueling studies in law, he still found the time to help those less fortunate. After graduation, Brad turned down many offers with prestigious law firms across the country. He moved to

Los Angeles to open his very own law firm. Brad still volunteers to help those who need it most.

My father claims that Brad has an open heart for those who have a hard time getting by in life. I countered my father's statement by jokingly telling him that Brad isn't doing the work with a big heart, but it's part of his evil plan to build a secret army of followers so he can eventually take over the world.

As you might have guessed by now, Nate and I are married. In June, we'll be enjoying our fortieth anniversary. We married after college and, years later, had two beautiful children, Rebecca and Evan.

Nate and I attended Georgia State University. You might find it strange, but Nate graduated with a degree in American History. Now you might be asking yourself, *wait a minute, you're telling me that a kid who leaped over fifty-three years of our American history holds a degree on the subject?* That's exactly right. After our return home, Nate developed a hunger for everything he missed. For years, his favorite pastime was spending countless hours at local libraries reading up on all the major American historical events. He decided to teach at the very same college that gave him his wings to fly.

What about me? Well, let's see, after I spent a great deal of time helping my father write his book, I took a few years to be a kid. I journeyed the twisting roads of my remaining teenage years. I earned high marks in school, which opened the doors for many top-notch universities. I ultimately decided to remain in Atlanta with my family.

I had taken a year off after high school. I needed a little time to reflect on the past and find some focus on the future. It had taken me some time to figure out what I wanted to do with the rest of my days. When I began attending college classes, I still wasn't sure of my direction. I had changed my major at least three times. What I finally set my sights on was naval architecture. To be a little more clarifying, I created original plans for sailboats.

During my time of reflection in college, I thought of what intrigued me the most in my twenty years of life. The answer was so obvious that it would have bitten me if it had teeth. Although it had taken a little time to reveal the inner desire to design incredible ships, I had found my calling.

The best part about it was that I could make my career anywhere in the world. I designed one-of-a-kind boats for each customer and left it up to the worthy engineers and builders of my company to bring the design to reality. My outlook on what made a boat beautiful poured into my designs. After I had done a spectacular work of art for an English billionaire, my work grabbed worldwide attention. It isn't surprising that I named my company *The Gateway Nautical Design Incorporated*. Soon my designs were selling faster than we could build them. I spent a little over thirty years in the profession. Now I'm retired and enjoying the remaining years of my life.

Nate retired from teaching a few years ago. We now spend a great deal of time traveling the world and seeing the incredible sights both God and man have created. To this day, neither of us travels by ship.

Whether or not Simora survived, we still acknowledge that a small group of humans bested her on her most wrathful day. We had found the means to escape. By our departure from that world, we also accepted the idea that Lothlora found victory and reclaimed the lands. To this day, I still believe that Graur and all of the other creatures of the land no longer feared the night. For me, that makes for a pretty good ending.

Every so often, I come across a newscast about a ship gone missing. Whether it's in the middle of the Atlantic, the Pacific, along the gulf coast, or even if it's far along the reaches of the Antarctica shoreline, I sometimes believe that maybe Simora is up to her wicked ways again.

"Grandma, are you coming?" Zoe asked from the kitchen doorway.

I don't know how long I was staring into the blackness of the kitchen window. I realized the sun had found its bed for the night.

I took Zoe's small hand.

"Show me the way, sweetie," I said.

We went out the sliding glass back door and onto the patio. A fire was dancing merrily in the stone pit. The sky was cloudless, and a million stars looked down on us. It was such a pleasant night to be outside.

"Here's a seat for you, mom," my daughter said as she patted the chair beside her.

My father and stepmother, unfortunately, couldn't make the trip. The rest of my family had come to enjoy our yearly reunion. With a family like this, I thought that probably makes me one of the richest people in the world.

"Well, let's see what you kids can do," Nate said as he poked giant marshmallows onto long metal prongs and handed them out to the grandchildren.

"I think I'm a little afraid to watch," Rebecca said with a chuckle.

"Don't cook them too much," Zoe warned the other children.

When the marshmallows were lightly blackened, slightly melted, we squashed them with a small chunk of chocolate between graham crackers and passed them around. We ate with obvious delight.

After finishing her third s'more, Sarah said, "Grandma, do you think you could tell us a story?"

I smiled at that. Of course, I have a lifetime of stories, but the children wanted to hear one in particular. It's a story I've been promising to share with all of the grandchildren for some time now. I've always wanted the moment for such a story to be just right.

This is a true story. I know because I lived it. So did Nate. My children have listened to this story numerous times. I still don't believe they've ever grown tired of it. It's the first time the grandchildren have heard the long tale that begins with a boat and a gateway made of light.

"She'd love to tell you a story," Nate said and winked at me.

With all of us nestled around the fire and beneath the stars, I began the tale as all good tales should begin.

"Once upon a time…"

Made in the USA
Monee, IL
04 March 2021

61971426R00135